COSTLY REFLECTIONS IN A MIDAS MIRROR

Iris Weil Collett and Dana Forgione

For me, a career in accounting has been like a day in a great orchard with ripe fruit on every tree and insufficient time to taste it all. Opportunities have been overwhelming. Rewards have been more than adequate. I think it will always be so.

—Robert K. Mautz

THOMAS HORTON AND DAUGHTERS
26662 S. NEW TOWN DRIVE
SUN LAKES, ARIZONA 85248

All characters, other than purely historical characters, and events in this book are fictitious and any resemblance to actual persons and events is coincidental.

Most companies, however, use management accounting information derived from the system used to prepare periodic financial statements. Driven by the procedures and cycles of the financial reporting system, most management accounting information is too aggregated, too distorted, and too delayed to be relevant for managerial planning and control. Today's management accounting systems rarely fit contemporary markets and technologies.
—H. Thomas Johnson and Robert S. Kaplan

We urge that in order to successfully serve in the dual role of managers/accountants, management accountants must be prepared to face the challenges of providing management with "classic" and "tailor-made" financial and nonfinancial information. They also must take advantage of the opportunities to expand and enhance their participation in the management process in "traditional" and "world-class" organizations.
—Grover L. Porter and Michael D. Akers

Dedicated to Arnold Marmor

Copyright © 1995 Thomas Horton and Daughters

No part of this work may be reproduced in any form without permission in writing from the publisher.

Library of Congress Catalog Card Number 94-077805

ISBN 0-913878-54-5

COSTLY REFLECTIONS IN A MIDAS MIRROR

Iris Weil Collett is back! Called a "cross between Mickey Spillane and Mr. Chips" by the *Washington Post*, Collett (a.k.a. D. Larry Crumbley) is the author of the four widely adopted novels, *The Ultimate Rip-off: A Taxing Tale*, *Accosting The Golden Spire*, *Trap Doors and Trojan Horses*, and *The Burmese Caper*. *Business Week* in June, 1989 called him a mover and shaker and said he "aims to lend excitement to the study of debits and credits by couching the stuff in romantic prose."

And this time he's teamed up with Dana Forgione for a sizzling new accounting thriller! *Costly Reflections* capitalizes on Forgione's special talents as a fraud examiner, CPA, management accountant, and university professor, all rolled into one! The characters take on the furtive air of a Mickey Spillane whodunit as they track down the calculating culprits.

Using forensic accountants as his major characters, Collett is truly the Mark Twain of the accounting profession. His goal is to spice up ho-hum subjects and to make students see that the accounting profession is much better than the stereotype image they have. According to the *Wall Street Journal*, his novels prove that the phrase "suspenseful accounting" is not necessarily an oxymoron.

Fortune, June 29, 1991, quoted Crumbley: "To be a good accountant, you have to be a good detective" and called his latest novel an "instructional thriller." Appearing on the front cover of the December 1988, issue of *Management Accounting* as a be-spectacled Mickey Spillane, Crumbley has gained recognition tantamount to "accounting man of the year." Kathy Williams, author of "The Case of the Purloined Pagoda" said to "move over Arthur Hailey." And *WG&L Accounting News* compared Collett to Indiana Jones.

PREFACE

Costly Reflections in a Midas Mirror is a supplementary text to be used near the end of a principles of managerial accounting course or at the beginning of a second-level cost accounting course. This instructional novel is ideal for an MBA program or finance course which has a light coverage of managerial accounting, or can be used in CPA firms' or IRS in-house training programs. It is also suitable for a law school course on managerial accounting.

Gerhard G. Mueller, past president of the American Accounting Association, indicates that "malaise" best describes accounting education today. "Our present textbooks and pedagogy haven't changed since the 1950's and are quite obsolete." A scenario approach is one answer to this malaise. A scenario is an example with a character (a person) performing certain actions in a particular situation.

The use of an imaginative novel is an ultimate extension of the scenario approach. A novel can be a series of continuous examples relating to a central theme instead of just several unrelated examples put forth as separate scenarios. In addition, students tend to relate to fictional characters in action-packed adventures. The story, along with its verbal pictures, jogs the memory more easily than gray pages of technical material alone. Proven aids in learning include the element of surprise when a learner encounters an unexpected phenomenon, and the retention of a new concept which appears in a dramatic, unusual context.

This novel mixes fraud, murder, art, ethics, and cost accounting together to get a better way of learning the accounting process. Lenny Cramer, a professor at Columbia

University, tries to help a wealthy friend of his university. As a managerial professor, he uses his forensic accounting background to solve a "whodunit" plot. Along the way, business practices and accounting concepts are elucidated in a way both students and instructors will find gripping as well as informative.

In 1976, L.G. Eckel penned the following:

There was an accountant
 who got in a stew
He had so many choices
He didn't know what to do.

The potential murderers are, likewise, numerous in this fast-paced Philip Marlowe-type intrigue. Although a fundamental premise in accounting is that the reporting entity is a going-concern in the absence of evidence to the contrary, with so many murders in this plot, a liquidation assumption is more appropriate. So jump on board and enjoy the read. But keep sunk cost values and salability of assets in mind as you unravel the plot, rather than the traditional historical costs. Remember that an effective managerial accountant must be a good detective, even without the fedora and snub-nosed revolver.

We wish to thank Ronald Bagley, Alan Blankley, Marc J. Epstein, Jeffrey Kantor, and Winston Shearon. A special thanks goes to Jean Ware, our dedicated typing and phone assistant.

Iris Weil Collett
Dana Forgione

One

Successful inventory management depends on the company's ability to efficiently control the movement of goods into an organization, through the organization and out of the organization.
—Murray Benenson

He was neatly dressed in a business suit even though it was obvious he was a bodyguard. He was tall and thin with brown hair and opaque eyes. He had a lean tightness about him that suggested a no-nonsense attitude. He was the kind you would want on your side in a street fight. If he was wearing a gun, it was cleverly concealed.

I followed him down the gray polished granite corridor to the door marked private. He knocked, keeping his eyes cautiously locked on me, and we both heard someone say, "Come in."

He opened the door, allowed me to enter, and then slowly closed the door. I could hear his fading footsteps as he walked away.

I stood in Henderson's office with my back against the closed door, taking in the functional office, taking in the polished black ebony furniture, taking in Henderson himself.

Lloyd Henderson.

Colossus.

Self-made, or sharply self-honed image? What's the difference? Not quite 70 but alert and alive in both mind and body.

The look of a savant. Eyes narrow like a cobra's. Wisps of white hair clinging to his small, narrow head. A small nose over a thin mouth. There was no chin, really. What would a big shot like Henderson want with a chin? I had done some quick checking as soon as John S. Burton, the President of my University, had told me about the situation and asked me to help out. Or rather Hildy, my secretary, had done the checking. Three daughters. Two living with him and one cast adrift. A modern King Lear.

His voice was raspy. "Professor Cramer? Lenny Cramer?" I nodded my head. He knew who I was. He had sent for me. Did he like playing games? He motioned to a chair. I walked to the chair and sat down slowly.

April was dying and soon it would be May, and Mr. Henderson wore a suit that was much too heavy for that kind of weather. Gray suit, white shirt, and red paisley tie. "Recently returned from the Cote d'Azur," he rasped. "Business. And what do I find? Problems."

I nodded my head in sympathy.

Henderson squinted at me. "This is a family matter. I want everything handled discreetly. No police involvement. Do you understand?"

"Sure, Mr. Henderson."

"How old are you, Professor Cramer?"

"Forty-three."

"A good reliable age. Do you drink?"

"Rarely." I wanted to tell him I drank sometimes, but I had the feeling he wouldn't like that answer.

"I never drink," he said. "It burns out your insides. Do you smoke?"

I was getting tired of off-the-point questions. But what could I do? "Never."

"Don't hold with smoking," he snapped. "I don't drink, and I don't smoke, and I'm fit as a fiddle."

"Why don't you tell me what's on your mind, Mr. Henderson?"

"I have a granddaughter," he said, "who is sort of wild. I haven't seen her in years. But I always had a soft spot in my heart for her. Her mother, my daughter Myra, came to see me yesterday. She claims Marilyn is mixed up with a sordid crowd. She's—uh—living with an artist. In Soho. I was rather surprised she showed up, my daughter, I mean. Haven't seen her in years. She cried like a baby, wanting my help. I promised I would. On the condition she would stay away from me."

"There's no blackmail involved in this is there?"

He frowned. "Blackmail? What makes you think that?"

"I don't think anything. Just asked. Wealthy men are vulnerable to blackmailers."

"I'm not being blackmailed, Professor. The very idea!" He was highly indignant.

"This daughter who came to see you—her name and address?"

He opened a drawer and gave me a slip of paper.

"And Marilyn's address?"

"You'll have to ask Myra," he said. "I told her I would get someone to help. I told her I would send him to her and she should talk to him. She operates a small art gallery."

"Are your other daughters aware of this—uh—family problem?" I said.

"You know something about me, do you? That I have three daughters?"

"You're a prominent man, Mr. Henderson. Wealthy people find their names constantly in the newspapers. And their backgrounds."

"My so-called shady deals," he cackled. "Well, news pulp innuendoes don't phase me. No, indeed. I have two daughters who stay with me and take care of me. The other one, Myra, she was *wild*, and I suppose Marilyn takes after her."

"Uh huh. Now, Mr. Henderson, you wouldn't have contacted John Burton just because Marilyn is mixed up with a wild crowd. There has to be more to it than that."

"You'll see Myra," he said stubbornly. "She'll tell you what you need to know."

"That young man who showed me to your office. He looks capable of handling any kind of problem."

"You mean Paul. Paul Manfred. Paul is my bodyguard. I don't send him out on such errands. Family matters. Besides, Paul is rather impulsive."

"If you don't have anything to do with your daughter, Myra, can you tell me what caused the rupture?"

"I don't see how that can possibly help you," he snapped, glaring. Then with a terse scowl, "Paul will see you *out*, Mr. Cramer."

I stood up, and took my leave. The building I was in was all Henderson's. He was into computers, and held several patents pertaining to silicon and metal-oxide based memory chips, and was wealthy, a modern Midas.

What was a Columbia accounting professor doing here? I made the mistake of telling the President at a university meeting about a year ago that I specialized in art work— hard assets. That was my mistake ... and his good memory.

Burton told me to help Henderson with a delicate family-related financial matter. Apparently Henderson had willed some of his art works to go to Columbia when he dies. He suggested I might get some consulting work with his computer company in return.

All of this on top of the fact I had to cut short my faculty leave because of a tooth problem. While on leave, I had taught principles of business in a private school in Odessa, in the Ukraine. Next, in Kiev, I taught accounting at another Institute. Also, another group called the Union of Economic Initiatives organized lectures for me throughout the Kiev area. Kiev is only 50 miles from that infamous Chernobyl nuclear power plant.

Since dentists make only 150 rubles (about $5 to $10) a month, dental care is very primitive. Two dentists, each with 6 years of experience, removed a filling from one of my healthy teeth. They refused to give me penicillin for my infected gums because they said it was very dangerous to take penicillin for more than six days. They put a temporary filling on the otherwise healthy tooth and said good-bye in Russian. That is when I decided to return to the States earlier than planned.

Everything was in short supply—housing, cars, food, medicine, surgical gloves, *etc.* In Odessa there was no water from midnight to 7:00 a.m., and hot water was sporadic most of the time. A shower was always a risk. It seemed that just when you were all lathered up, the hot water would disappear without notice. Some cities only have water eight to 10 hours per day. What can you expect, I thought, from a system which has no profit incentive? As I had told my Soviet audiences, there are only three ways to motivate people: by love, by profit, or by guns. Socialistic and communistic systems work only for primitive, agricultural societies, if then, and not in our modern industrial countries.

My tooth had started hurting during my lecture on break-even analysis. As I told the Ukrainian students, the break-even point is the number of units that must be sold in order for the total revenue from the sales of a product to equal the total costs of production.

Oh, I had drawn the typical break-even chart on an overhead transparency which I had taken with me; transparencies were in short supply also. A transparency marker could probably not even be found.

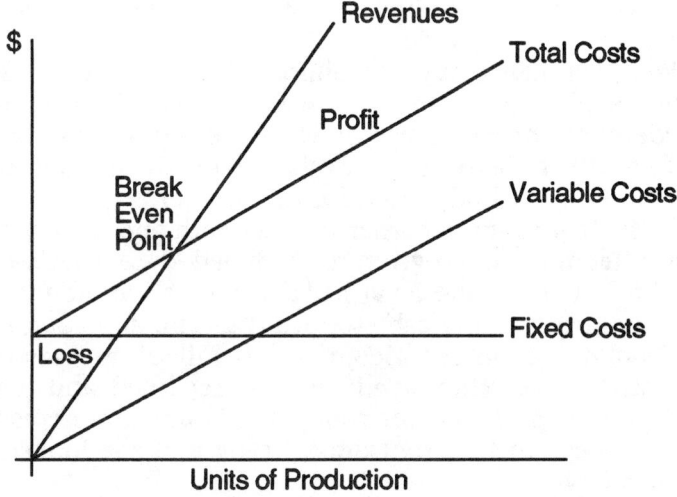

I'm not sure they had understood the concept of "relevant range." That variable costs and fixed costs can be identified only for a certain range of activity.

Or I wasn't sure that they understood the nice formulas I had worked.

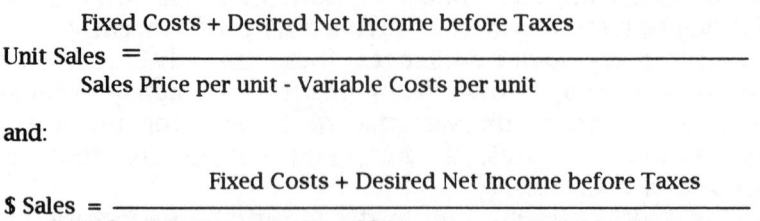

and:

$$\$ \text{ Sales} = \frac{\text{Fixed Costs} + \text{Desired Net Income before Taxes}}{(\text{Sales Price per unit} - \text{Variable Costs per unit}) / \text{Sales Price per unit}}$$

I still remember how perplexed they looked when I explained that they should continue producing units as long as the revenue from sales of those extra units covered their own variable costs, plus at least $1 of fixed costs. Of course, over the long run, all fixed costs must be covered in full by sales of the company's product if it's going to stay in business. But, on a short-run basis, any contribution toward coverage of the fixed costs will improve profits—or reduce company losses. Did they even understand the meaning of "profit?"

Well, enough day dreaming. How could I solve Henderson's problem? I wasn't even sure what Henderson's problem was. Well, it certainly wouldn't be solved with break-even analysis—or by whispering sweet debits into somebody's ear, for that matter.

Outside, I found a corner phone booth and took out the paper Henderson had given me. I dialed Myra Riley's number. I told her I would be at her place in half an hour.

The third cruising cab stopped. I got in, and soon I was in Brooklyn. Brooklyn Heights was full of brownstones. The street Mrs. Riley lived on was tree-lined and looked fairly well kept. I paid the cabby and bounced up crescent-shaped steps to the front door. I rang and she looked out the window.

"Push in the door, Mr. Cramer, and come up."

I did so. She met me at the head of the stairs. She was somewhere in her early forties, dressed in well-tailored, yet slightly worn, red slacks and a cotton shirt. We went into her apartment. Much better than the flat where I stayed in Odessa only weeks before. Odessa, Ukraine, not Odessa, Texas.

The living room was comfortable, with graceful furniture, and a number of oil paintings on the walls.

We sat and she told me she was a widow and had kept her husband's name. She told me she didn't know what to do about Marilyn.

"Exactly what is the problem?" I said.

"This is so ... embarrassing."

"It usually is."

"Would you like a drink?"

"No. What exactly is the problem?" So far, my time would have been better spent working in my office on that never-ending research paper.

If she had a handkerchief in her hands she would have torn it to shreds, she was that nervous. "Marilyn is 20. She likes to think she's an adult. Of course, legally, she is, but mentally—well, she acts like a child. She doesn't know her own mind. She's always been a problem to me—"

"She's 20 and she's an adult," I said. "You went to your father for help. What kind of help?"

"I own a small art gallery. Marilyn helps me in the gallery. She does all the bookkeeping. I believe she may be taking money from the shop." She paused for a moment. "But I have no proof."

One person controlling the books—typical small business. Inwardly, I shook my head. The first principle of internal control is *separation of duties*. Never let the same person safeguard the cash and keep the books—there's too much temptation and opportunity for embezzlement. It even happens among family members. When two or more people divide the financial tasks, any misappropriation of funds requires collusion. Of course, workers might collude, but the more people that are involved, the less likely it is that a "successful" collusion will occur.

I knew of an organization that allowed the same treasurer to control all of it's finances for more than forty years. During the latter years of his career he developed significant medical problems that were very costly to treat. He had a need, and he had more than abundant opportunity to steal. Oddly, when a new president took office, some uncomfortable financial questions were raised, and over the course of two months, a total of $240,000 appeared out of nowhere in the company's cash accounts. No sales, no transfers from other accounts, and no loan proceeds could account for the influx. Apparently, the treasurer decided to put it all back. Or, maybe he just borrowed enough money to cover the obvious losses—and to quiet the questions—while he waited for opportunities to steal the money again in order to pay back his creditors.

Not likely that Marilyn would run a sophisticated embezzlement scheme. But then again, what how much did I know about Marilyn Riley?

Myra's eyes were fixed on mine. "She's involved with this ... boy. He's an artist. He's on drugs. She's poses for him. And—and—"

She looked away.

"Marilyn was involved in a theft. She'll go to jail. I'm so afraid—"

"How do you know?" I leaned forward.

"She boasted about it," Myra Riley said. "She was here, just two days ago, and boasted about stealing. I think she was drunk. If she's caught—she'll go to jail. She's my daughter. She's out of control, but I love her."

"What sort of stealing? Art from your shop? Money from your cash receipts?"

"She didn't do the actual stealing herself. It was her boyfriend, Teddy Noren. He works part-time in the gallery."

"Did you tell your suspicions to your father?"

"Sure. He's always liked Marilyn. I was sure he would help. I have no real money, Mr. Cramer, and I knew I would need help. A lawyer or a private detective."

"I'm not a detective, just a forensic accounting professor. Now what was stolen? I may be able to help."

"I don't know. She didn't say. She mentioned something about it being worth a half-million dollars."

"Did you question her about it?"

"Of course. It was useless. She just giggled like when she was a little girl, and then took off."

"You think this Teddy Noren is involved?"

"Oh, I'm sure of it. They're very close friends, you know. I'm so worried."

"You'd better take something for your nerves," I advised. "You can't go to pieces. You won't be helping your daughter that way." I leaned back and stretched. "Do you have Teddy Noren's address and phone number? I'll have to pay him a visit."

"The address book. It's in the kitchen." She went to get it, and came back with a pad and pencil and the address book. She found the address and number and wrote it down.

"Your daughter there now?"

"I don't know. Could be. Or she could be working somewhere for some artist. She poses in her free time."

"What caused you and your father to split up?" I asked.

"I don't see—"

"Just curious."

"I met George Riley and I fell in love with him. My father said he was a fortune hunter. I think he just wanted me to stay at home and take care of him. He's like that. He uses his illnesses to control ... all of us. Me and my two sisters. I couldn't live that way. I insisted on marrying George and so he disinherited me. After my husband died I tried to see my father, but he wouldn't have it. I visited him several times during later years, but he always made it unpleasant. I never asked him for anything. Just—just to see him, to remind him he had another daughter besides the two witches who stayed with him. The only reason he even talked to me the other day was because Marilyn was in trouble."

"You don't get along with your sisters?"

"We hate each other. I think Cora and Sandra hate each other. Oh, what's the difference. He's a very spiteful, vindictive man, Professor Cramer. I think the three of them love their mutually exploitive existence in that ... house."

"Yes." I stood up. "What's the difference."

Two

Managers need not—and should not—abandon the effort to justify computer integrated manufacturing on financial grounds. Instead, they need ways to apply the discounted cash flow approach more appropriately.

—Robert S. Kaplan

I had lunch in a coffee shop on Metropolitan Avenue and then a cab took me back to Manhattan. The weather was mild and people were starting to wear summer clothes. We were in Soho now, and the driver kept an eye peeled for Prince Street.

"Easier to get around here than in the Village," he said. "Here we are."

It was a four story, dingy brown brick building crammed between an art gallery and a store that specialized in silver jewelry. A whiff of back-alley stench greeted me as I walked into the building. One of the mail boxes had a faded card taped near it which read Noren/Riley. The number 12 was on the card. I went up three flights of filthy stairs. A crack dealer's heaven, I thought to myself. Number 12 was slightly ajar. There was the faint smell of cordite.

"Trouble?" I said half out loud and pushed the door open with my elbow. When I was inside I pushed the door back with my other elbow.

Half the living room had been converted into an art studio. There was an easel, a painting resting on it, a nearby table with tubes of paint, brushes, small pallet knives for textured painting, and rags. I saw a couple of small bottles of linseed oil. A chair had been overturned. On the floor between the chair and the easel lay the body of a young man. He was on his left side, his face turned up with dispassionate, stark eyes—a face that was rigid, framed with short-cropped brown hair. He was dressed in baggy black pants. His chest and feet were white and bare. He looked like a fellow who had fallen asleep with his eyes open. There was just the faintest trickle of blood coming from his right temple. Near his hand was the gun—a .38 revolver.

No sign of a struggle. It looked like he was sitting on the chair and then, for reasons known only to him, aimed the gun at his head and pulled the trigger. So he was on the floor from the force of the bullet, and the chair went with him. Looked like a clear case of suicide.

Now what was the problem?

I looked at the painting. Suicide. It didn't make sense. I touched the tip of my little finger to a corner, and it was slightly wet. The brush strokes were short and uncertain. I thought I recognized the subject. A fresh forgery? Possibly. But, sometimes artists train by copying great masterpieces.

I looked at the tubes of paint. I mindlessly started rolling them around on the table.

Then I went through the rest of the apartment. No more tubes of paint. I was getting edgy now. Suicide would suit me fine—no mess, no problems. I went through the apartment again. It wasn't a big apartment. Living room, bedroom, kitchen, and a bathroom. I even looked under the bed and, that made me feel foolish. But I was getting a bit frantic. I wanted it to be suicide. The only items in the bedroom that didn't seem to belong were two laboratory type balance scales. An open package of grocery store paraffin—old-fashioned white laundry wax—on top of the dresser. A couple of half-inch sized chunks of paraffin sitting on one of the scales.

Where was Marilyn? Posing? Shopping? I couldn't stay in the apartment, not with a dead body for company.

I used my handkerchief to wipe off everything I might have touched and went downstairs. I walked into the nearby art gallery.

There was a painting that took up an entire wall. It was an abstract mess. Smaller paintings hung on other walls. Acrylics, oils, and a few watercolors. A young woman in her 20's, wearing a black blazer over black leggings and a pair of Doc Martens gave me a smile. She pointed to a table which carried a bottle of white wine and some paper cups. I shook my head, no.

"I'm looking for somebody," I said. "Marilyn Riley. Maybe you know her. She lives next door."

"If she lives next door," the girl said, "why don't you go up and see her?"

"No one home."

"Well, how can I help you?"

"If you know her ..."

"I know Marilyn."

"Do you have any idea where she could be now?"

"She's probably at her mother's art gallery or with a photographer. Isn't Teddy home? Teddy Noren. Her significant-other."

"I knocked and there was no answer," I lied.

The girl was getting obviously bored. "What do you want me to do about it?"

"I wonder if you'd mind answering a few questions. I'm not a cop. Just someone who's looking for her."

"I believe I do mind, Mr. ..."

"Stanley. J.D. Stanley." Lying always made me feel uncomfortable.

"Mr. Stanley, I'm afraid I can't help you. I know Marilyn, and I know Teddy. I like them. And I don't like snoops. Now if you'll excuse me."

"I'm not a snoop."

"All right," she said. "So you're not a snoop. Now will you kindly leave?"

Sometimes you have a hit, but sometimes you strike out. I had struck out.

I made a slight bow. "Whatever you like. One question that can't hurt anyone. Is there an art supply store near here?"

"Walk up to West Broadway, and turn right one block."

"Thank you." I made my retreat.

If the police questioned her, she would remember me. Even if the cops decided it was suicide they would question her, as a neighbor. Routine. And they would look for Marilyn Riley, the dead man's lover. I wanted to see Marilyn before the police arrived.

I had some luck at the art supply store. Sketch pads, china pencils, brushes, easels, paints, *etc.* All high volume items. There are two basic strategies in retail operations—high turnover, low margin, or low turnover, high margin. Turnover is the speed with which an item of inventory moves through a business. That is, the amount of time it takes from receipt of an item from a supplier 'til the item is sold to a customer. Discount stores depend on high turnover of merchandise inventory, while hospitals suffer from slow turnover of accounts receivable.

The same turnover concept applies to all balance sheet items, since they can all be thought of as "inventories"—that is, inventory of cash, inventory of merchandise, inventory of receivables, inventory of equipment, *etc.* Both the fast and slow turnover strategies can be equally efficient from a Return on Investment standpoint, but you've got to match the strategy with the nature of the product market. In an art supply store like the one I was in, a high margin, slow turnover strategy would leave the owner with few sales, and a lot of dried-out paint sitting on the shelves. It was a crowded place and there were artists and students looking at things, buying supplies. I finally cornered a middle-aged looking gentleman. Balding, slight, with glasses.

"Teddy Noren recommended me," I told the salesman.

"Oh, yes. Mr. Noren. A nice chap. Good artist. I've seen his work."

"He said he gets all his oils from you."

The salesman reflected. "Oils? He never buys oils from here. Acrylic. That's what he uses mostly, as far as I know."

I thanked the man and left.

Back to Myra Riley. She had an anxious look on her face. Her nerves were considerably worse. We sat down, facing each other. "Marilyn isn't home," I said.

"You could have called me," she said.

"You didn't see Teddy Noren today, did you?"

Her face dropped to a sharp frown. "What? Of course not. What kind of question is that?"

I looked at her, and said, "Mind if I have a glass of water?" She turned without answering, and I watched her go to the kitchen.

She handed me the glass, and sat down again. She hadn't made a drink for herself. "Why did you ask if I had seen Teddy today?"

"Just asking. I was in his apartment. You're sure he's on drugs?"

"Yes. Absolutely."

"I didn't see Marilyn, either."

"Did you talk to Teddy?" she said anxiously.

"I tried. I wanted to. But he was sort of tongue tied. You know how it is when you're dead."

She gasped. Her face went ashen white.

"It looked like a suicide," I said.

"Suicide?" She was regaining control. Gulped. "Suicide? But he was so young. What reason would he have?"

"I don't know. I didn't know the man. I didn't know his problems, his frustrations. Nothing."

"Where does this leave Marilyn?" she asked.

"Where does it leave me? I was in his apartment. Somebody might have seen me go into the building. What if the police find me and ask me questions? What do I tell them?"

"You tell them nothing," she said crisply. "They can't force you to tell them anything, can they?"

"Are you a lawyer?" I asked.

"No."

"Then I guess they can," I said.

She wrung her hands, and I wondered if she knew Teddy Noren was dead when she gave me his address.

"Was there a theft?" I said, wanting to get back to the reason I got involved in this whole thing in the first place.

She was angry now. "I told you, didn't I? What are you trying to say?"

"You don't know what was stolen?"

"No. I don't see—"

I stood up. "We'll postpone it, Mrs. Riley, for now. I want to see Marilyn—before the police do."

She also stood up and stepped close to me, closer than she had to. She took my glass. "I think you should call me Myra."

"All right, Myra."

"If Marilyn should call—"

"Have her call me. I'll leave you my business card."

"And you mustn't think I'm holding out on you," she said. "I am being honest with you."

"Of course."

"There's doubt in your voice, Lenny," she observed.

"A natural inclination because of the business I'm in. Accountants live with a healthy skepticism. I'll call you this evening."

She saw me to the door. I couldn't place the perfume; Passion, I think.

I went down and took a cab to my office on campus—four cabs passed by before one finally stopped.

Three

Although the calculation of standard costs are still important, we now emphasize the different levels at which standards can be set, the motivational impact of having standards, the behavioral consequences of either favorable or unfavorable variances, and the impact of changing standards on workers and management.
—R. L. Benke and R. H. Hermanson

18. What type of cost will change in direct proportion to changes in activity level?
    a. sunk cost
    b. fixed cost
    c. variable cost
    d. opportunity cost
    e. none of above

   I circled "c. variable cost," the correct answer. I was reviewing the cost accounting examination I would give to my students at the end of the week. As usual on a multi-choice exam, the correct answer was c.

   I had to be more careful. On a multi-choice exam with five possible answers, a person with no knowledge should be able to score 20 points. With the knowledge that c was the most frequent answer, even a fine arts major could score more than 20 points on a cost accounting exam because of the law of averages.

   I replaced my pocket calendar and the map into my brown leather brief case. The one I purchased in Hong Kong. It reminded me of Dana Scott and my Burma episode. Painful memories of my first love after the death of my wife came rushing back. Dana was still in prison for her attempt to steal the treasures from the Burma stupa in

Rangoon. That seemed a long time ago. I wish I could get back to Thailand.

I finished proofing the cost accounting examination, and hid it in my bottom, left-hand drawer. After retrieving my teaching notes, I left my office on the sixth floor and took the elevator to the Watson library on the first floor. Uris Hall has eight floors. The business library is well-maintained and well-staffed.

I had left my October 1991 issue of **Management Accounting** at home, so I checked it out from the library. In this issue Robert Koehler asserts that a combination of activity-based costing, direct costing, and the contribution margin approach will give a true overview of the whole cost picture. Well, that's certainly an improvement anyway, I concluded. So often cost reports get distorted by including allocated indirect, noncontrollable costs using blunt and arbitrary methods. Few things are more frustrating and futile than holding managers responsible for costs over which they have little or no control. John Burton would be wasting his time if he tried to hold faculty members like me responsible for cost control on the construction of that new Northside parking garage at the University. Sorry, but faculty members just don't have any control or authority over parking garage construction costs. While activity-based costing is a major refinement of indirect cost allocation methods, it nonetheless still boils down to arbitrary decisions about what business activities *drive* what costs, and how to measure and apply those cost relationships in practice.

Product pricing decisions based on unit costs that embody over or under-allocations of cost, compared to the actual cost necessary for production of that product, can have devastating effects on the price-competitiveness of an entire company. That is, if production of a certain titanium jet engine part requires three machine-tool set-ups, but only one direct labor hour, then using the antiquated standard of *direct labor hours* to apply overhead costs will understate the actual cost of making that product. Prices based on cost will then be too low and the company will unwittingly lose money on sales of the jet engine part.

Number of machine-tool set-ups should be used as the cost driver for allocating costs to the jet engine part—especially if the cost of a machine-tool set-up is more than the cost of one direct labor hour.

I then headed for my afternoon class.

As Professor Lenny Cramer, I began my lecture by clearing my throat. Conversations among the students slowly settled down, and came to a halt. I casually scanned the motley aggregation of students in the cost accounting class.

With a low, quiet voice I stated, "You all, of course, have read the chapter and done your homework for today."

Some students nodded their heads. Many looked rather uninterested in the way this class—every class—had begun. Some students were reading the **Columbia Daily Spectator**, the 15 cent student newspaper.

As the room became quiet, I asked louder. "My first question, then, is what is a *variable* cost? Pretend I'm your friend majoring in art history. How would you explain variable costs to me?"

A heavy-set young man on the front row raised his hand. I nodded in his direction. "Yes," I said.

"Variable costs are costs that change in relation to increases or decreases in an activity, such as units of production."

I smiled. "Exactly. What are some examples?"

The student responded, "Direct material costs usually increase as units of production increase; so, they would be classified as a variable cost. On the other hand, a supervisor's salary is constant, it wouldn't change with fluctuations in units of production."

"Good. So what kind of cost is the supervisor's salary then?"

"Fixed cost," responded the student.

"Does everyone agree with that answer?" I asked the class at large.

A few students nodded. The majority of the class responded with blank looks on their faces.

"OK, let's take a vote. How many agree that a cost that doesn't change with fluctuations in an activity level is a *fixed* cost? Raise your hand if you agree."

Most students raised a hand.

I continued. "So, most of you agree that the supervisor's salary is a *fixed* cost. Therefore, the supervisor's salary never changes, no matter what the production level."

A number of students nodded their heads, but one student in the back of the room raised her hand.

"Yes? What is it?" I asked, looking toward her sitting in the right, rear corner of the large classroom.

"Well, Dr. Cramer, as I recall from our reading, a fixed cost is fixed only in relation to a given period of time and a specific range of activity."

"Excellent. That's exactly right. While the supervisor's salary is considered a fixed cost, when the production level increases beyond a certain level, then the firm will have to hire a second supervisor. Hiring a second supervisor would about double the amount of cost allocated to supervisor's salaries. For example, a manufacturing company running one assembly line eight hours a day, might only need one foreman. If the firm expands to running two eight-hour shifts, then they will need to hire a second foreman to supervise the second shift. That's known as a "step" cost. It increases in discrete "chunks" like the steps of a staircase. Can anyone think of another reason a fixed cost like the supervisor's salary would change?"

A student sitting in the middle of the room spoke out. "If it's a good union, they'll negotiate higher pay for the foreman at the next collective bargaining session." A number of students chuckled at the remark.

I smiled. "You've made a good point. Changes often occur in *fixed* costs over time. As you said, the union may bargain for a higher compensation package in their next contract. The rent on a building is generally considered a fixed cost relative to production, but from year to year, it is a negotiable item, depending on the lease term."

"What is meant by average fixed cost per unit and *total* fixed cost?" I asked.

The student on the front row, who had responded to the initial question, raised his hand.

I nodded in his direction again. The student began, "The total amount paid to the supervisor in a given period is the total cost for supervisor's salary. If we divide that amount by the number of units produced, we get the average cost per unit. Since a supervisor's salary is fixed, the total cost doesn't change if the level of production goes up *or* down. On the other hand, the average cost per unit of supervisor's salary will go up or down as the production level decreases or increases."

"Excellent. There is an inverse relationship between an average fixed cost per unit of activity and the level of activity, such as units of production. What about total and average *variable* costs?"

A second-row student raised a hand this time.

I motioned toward the student with my right hand. She responded. "Average variable cost per unit stays the same no matter what the production level. The total variable cost increases or decreases as the production level increases or decreases."

"Great!" I retorted. "Average *variable* cost per unit is constant as the activity level changes, but total *variable* cost changes in direct proportion to changes in the activity level."

I was happy. I loved to teach students who would respond actively to questions in the classroom. But students seem to study less and less each year. There had been severe grade inflation over the years, no doubt because of the widespread use of faculty evaluations.

I was constantly amazed at the reduction of coverage by professors as they attempted every trick in the book to increase their evaluations. One professor had once told me "to entertain them, reduce coverage, make it easy, and make them think they have learned something. That's the key. Make them think they've learned something. Obviously, easy examinations are essential."

I tried to teach students how to use the material they learned and relate it to real life. Cost, or managerial accounting gave students the analytic tools they needed to solve unstructured business problems. I emphasized different types of problem solving rather than rote calculations.

Since I know the left side of the brain will most often dominate, I try to get my students to use the right side of their brain with the use of vivid metaphors, parables, pictures, loud noises, and colors. I use examples of real business stories from my own experience, and require my students to read a cost accounting action-novel. I told my students that "half the brain of every student is virtually neglected. The *left* side of the brain understands technology and the *right* side sees how it fits into the total picture."

To try to encourage whole brain thinking—right plus left side—I always flash the following overhead on the screen during my first class period:

LEFT SIDE	RIGHT SIDE
▪ logical side	▪ creative side
▪ verbalizes	▪ nonverbal
▪ analyzes	▪ intuition
▪ abstracts	▪ leaps of insight
▪ marks time	▪ dreaming
▪ counts	▪ understands metaphors
▪ plans	▪ subjective
▪ makes rational statements on logic	▪ relational
	▪ holistic
	▪ time-free mode
	▪ creates new combinations of ideas

During examinations I leave the following overhead on the screen:

- I am not a bean counter.
- I have imagination.
- I will use the right side of my brain!
- I am creative.
- I will be a forensic accountant.

Three or four times during the exam I ask my students to hold their finger on their right nostril and breath through the left nostril. Breathing through the left nostril will stimulate the right side of the brain—or so I'm told. Even though there were generally more female than male students in accounting classes, I do not tell my students that the brain stem cap (the corpus callosum) of a mature female was significantly larger than in the male brain. In fact, we all start out with a female-sized brain stem cap, but gradually the male hormones shrink the male brain stem cap.

The female is probably better able to use both left brain and right brain in concert. There is greater communication between the right and left hemisphere in women, and they use both sides cooperatively, while men rely more directly on each side for distinct purposes. Therefore, the male is more easily trained to use mostly the left brain. He thinks more sequentially, while she thinks more associatively, but, of course, there are always exceptions.

Some experts suggest that left-handers and ambidextrous people have larger corpus callosum. With better communication, lefties divide their linguistic and spatial tasks between both hemispheres. Since I was right-handed, I figured these so-called experts must be left-handed.

We love closure, but in forensic accounting that can be risky. One of my finance professor friends at the University of Pennsylvania once told me that since accountants wore green eye shades, he didn't know if accountants had a right brain.

My claim to fame was forensic accounting or litigation support services. The American Institute of Certified Public Accountants defines a forensic accountant as a fraud auditor or investigative accountant who searches for evidence of criminal conduct or assists in the determination of, or rebuttal of, claimed damages. Much of my outside income was from plaintiffs and their lawyers. They hired me to provide investigative accounting services, prepare financial analyses in support of their case, and serve as an expert witness in the courtroom. I was a formidable opponent for the other attorney to cross-examine. It paid well, but took a pretty thick hide. It was not a sideline for the faint-hearted.

Now I did more than just disputed divorce-settlement work. My areas included antitrust analysis, general consulting, and cost allocation. Anytime someone had to dig into the corpse of records, I was available. Super accountant Cramer! Maybe I should get a special cape to wear like Superman. Or was that Batman? I pack an HP 12-C pocket calculator.

❂❂❂

I thought of Rebecca on my subway trip across town to my second office. As I left Atlanta to accept an endowed accounting chair at Columbia University, my 17 year old daughter became a freshman at Drake University, in Des Moines. She was a computer and business major. Not an accountant yet like her dad. She had called me last night from the Dial Computer Center, where she was doing some homework on the VAX—Drakes' large mainframe computer. She was probably checking out the boys, also. I chuckled as I got off the subway, and thought of my old days as a cyberian pinhead—what we used to affectionately call the students who just ate bags of salted peanuts from the vending machine and ran boxes of dot-matrix printout all night long on the CDC Cyber 150 mainframe. Fun times.

Four

Today, the scene is changing. Once again, managers are beginning to manage their companies rather than just the numbers. Many are doing it to survive, others because they recognize they must adapt to the new manufacturing environment if they are to maintain their competitive edge.
—C. J. McNair and William Mosconi

John Grant, with his skeletal face, sat behind his desk, hands folded in front of him, and listened to what I had to say. He was close to 60, thin as a reed, but wiry and active. John was the principal owner of a small forensic accounting practice, specializing in business fraud-related examinations. I was a silent partner, so I had done some consulting with his firm on numerous occasions.

"Look John, I don't have time for this project. I need you to help me." I told him the few details I knew.

"You think this Myra Riley just gave you a line and nothing else?" he quizzed. "What would be the point?"

"I don't know."

"She might be telling the truth."

"I'll know more when I talk to the daughter."

"Well, Mrs. Riley's father is paying the bills," Grant said. "And he is Lloyd Henderson. *The* Lloyd Henderson. He's a rich man—and a heavy donor to your school. We don't question his daughter's veracity as long as he keeps paying the bills. What makes you think her boyfriend was murdered?"

"The painting he had just finished," I said. "Or was supposed to be working on. The canvas was still wet. I touched it. Oil. A poor forgery of Bellini's Madonna. But all the tubes of paint on his table were acrylic. The brush strokes didn't look experienced enough for a struggling artist. I went through the apartment. No tubes of oils. Acrylic dries fast. I checked an art supply store where he gets his paint. He always buys acrylic. Somebody worked on that canvas. That somebody brought his own case of oils, worked on the canvas, then left. Before or after murdering Teddy Noren. There were bottles of linseed oil there—linseed is used to thin oil paints."

"Doesn't have to be murder," Grant snapped.

"Doesn't have to be. Right. So call it a feeling."

"And if it was murder, why should the killer work on a canvas in Noren's apartment."

"I don't know. Maybe to establish some kind of an alibi. At this point, I don't know."

"This person would have to be pretty stupid. The police would have experts that see the painting was a forgery. So, how much do you tell Henderson?"

"Myra Riley is my client," I said. "But if I do have to see Henderson, I will."

I went to a small office, passed the secretary, Hildy, who was busy on the phone, and gave her a wink. I kept a desk at the accounting firm. Actually I was a 15% silent partner. My department head at Columbia didn't know I led a double life: Professor by day, forensic accountant in the evening. Maybe one day there would be a television action series about me, say "The Manhattan Accountants." After all, there was a series called, "L.A. Law." Certainly an accountant led a more exciting life than a lawyer.

Our office was slightly different from most accounting offices. With a number of personal and business fraud cases, our investigators made use of computers, 9-track tape drives, and on-line data bases. Our investigators can comb dozens of on-line data bases such as credit reports, probate records, motor-vehicle registrations, and a number of electronic bulletin boards. We can load government mag tapes, right off their mainframes onto our PC workstations.

She came into the office a few minutes later. Hildy was about 40, with brown hair. Her skirt was lime green, and her blouse was lemon yellow. She sat down and said, "So you met the great Henderson, did you? What was your impression?

"A ruthless character. He lives for money."

"It seems to me he could have retired years ago, but that probably wouldn't suit a character like him. He works to make more money, more millions. I certainly wouldn't want to cross him in a business deal." Hildy said.

"How much do you know about him? And where did you learn it all?"

Hildy snorted. "You spend too much time in the ivory tower Lenny. From what I've read he controls his public image carefully. I suspect that when he's not grinding out the millions, he stays at home, with two of his devoted daughters."

"His third daughter was thrown out," I said. "King Lear and his three daughters."

"That's about it, Professor. Someone once wanted to do an unauthorized biography of him. Word got to Henderson. After all, that someone had to ask a lot of questions. That someone ended up in a hospital. Two broken legs. Somebody evidently explained Henderson's position to him in a back alley. There went the biography."

"And nothing proven against Henderson?"

"Fight the rich and powerful?" Hildy lifted her well shaped eyebrows, hazel eyes twinkling, "The idealists are dying out."

"Do me a favor, will you Hildy? Order a turkey sandwich and a Pepsi from the deli downstairs. Better have them bring it up."

"Sure." She got up. "Large or small?"

"Anything, thanks."

I thought and waited for the food ... and a phone call. When the food arrived I ate my sandwich and drank my dose of caramel colored phosphoric acid and caffeine. Sugar load. Then the phone rang.

A feminine voice, frightened. "Mr. Cramer?"

I asked if it was Marilyn.

"Yes. My mother—"

"Don't say anymore. Are you in your apartment on Prince Street?"

"Yes."

"Get over here right away." I gave her the address and hung up.

She was here in less than half an hour.

Marilyn Riley, granddaughter of the Lloyd Henderson. A blue-eyed blonde of 20, tall and slim, wearing loose jeans and a man's black dress shirt sat down. The shaken fright on her face was a dreadful thing to see.

"He's dead, Mr. Cramer. Teddy's dead."

"You walked in, found him, and called your mother. Is that right?"

"Yes."

"Did you call the police?"

"No. I'll have to, won't I?"

"Yes. But not yet."

Puzzled she said, "What do you mean?"

"I want to talk to you first."

"About what? Teddy's dead. I saw the gun—"

"Ever seen that gun before?"

"Yes. It's Teddy's."

"Did he ever talk to you about suicide?"

"Suicide? No. But I guess—"

"What time did you leave the apartment?"

"This morning? About nine."

"Was anyone else in the apartment beside Teddy?"

"No."

"Was he expecting anyone?"

"Well, he said he might meet Bram Walker for lunch. I guess he didn't."

"Who's Bram Walker?"

"A friend of ours. He paints—or at least he tries to. Landscapes. And other things."

"Oils or acrylic?"

"Oils." She sighed. "I don't see—"

"When you visited your mother, you told her you were involved in a theft."

She bit her lower lip. "My mother can be a pain. Let's just say she's not real keen on my life style. So I thought I'd—"

I interrupted her again. "Then there was no theft?"

"No, of course not. I was only teasing her."

"Very well. Go back to the apartment, call the police, and tell them you got home and found Teddy Noren dead. I would appreciate it if you didn't mention my part in this affair, Miss Riley."

"What do I do then, Mr. Cramer?"

"You can just go on with your life, Miss Riley. Since there was no theft, and you aren't in any trouble, you don't really need my services."

She looked bewildered by my remark.

"Your mother thought you were in trouble," I explained. "She went to her father, your grandfather. He called the President of my university, and I went to see your grandfather. He gave me your mother's number. I called her and saw her, and she told me you were involved in a theft. Some mothers worry, you know. Since there is no defalcation, and since you aren't in any trouble, then my services aren't required. It's as simple as that."

"Then why all the questions before?"

"Just wanted to make sure it was suicide. Probably is."

"You have reason to doubt it was suicide?" She couldn't understand that one. "It was Teddy's gun. I guess he killed himself. I don't see why he should. But—well, sometimes a person's mind goes over the edge."

There was no fright now. It had disappeared. She was rather composed. I wondered if she was relieved that Teddy was dead.

"I don't know if I could face the police alone," she said hesitantly.

"Call your mother first," I said. "Then the cops. Your mother can hold your hand while you give the police your story."

She bridled at this. "Oh, I see. No client, no money. So the sarcasm sets in." She smiled sweetly like a cobra before it strikes. "Why don't you string my mother along?" She got up in a huff. "Sorry there's no fees in it for you. But I don't think you can expect repeat business once the client is dead."

I didn't answer her. No retort. Nothing. I just wanted her to leave. She went and I had a bad taste in my mouth. I worked on several projects for the rest of the afternoon. I was actually productive.

A client came in to see Grant. I told Hildy I was through for the day and left. I stepped into a cramped restaurant and had dinner. Then I went home and to bed. No dreaming, at least none that I recall.

Teddy Noren's so-called suicide was on page six in the local newspaper. There wasn't much to it. Young artist takes own life. Marilyn Riley was mentioned. She had been his close friend. The reporter who had written the story hadn't connected her with Lloyd Henderson.

I read the paper on the way to my accounting office. Hildy tore off a sheet from a memo pad as I walked in the door. "Mr. Henderson called. He wants you to call him. A.S.A.P. He's at his home."

In my office, seated behind my gray Steelcase desk, I rang the number Hildy had given me. The voice was familiar. It was Paul Manfred. He transferred me to Henderson.

"Can you come right over, Dr. Cramer?"

"Something up?"

"Long Beach. Take the train." He could be demanding. "Paul will be there at the station. He's patient, Dr. Cramer. He'll wait until you get there." End of conversation. *Click.*

There was a click. I don't like being ordered around. I fumed silently for about 30 seconds and slammed the receiver down. Money. Money talks, money beckons. Greed, power ...

I went in to Grant's office and told him about Lloyd Henderson's call.

"Go see him," Grant said. "Never keep a wealthy client waiting."

"I had a feeling you might say that."

I caught a train from Penn Station. What a pit. Always filthy, smelly, crime-ridden. The conduit of a seemingly endless torrent of every imaginable type of human existence—and the late-night haunt of all the bizarre urban cast-offs. The city's sad display-case of tragic human pathology. I had hoped that I was through with the Hendersons and the Rileys. What was up now?

Paul Manfred was waiting at the station in Long Beach. Leaning against the glossy fender of an armored black stretch limo. He nodded and held the rear door open for me. I climbed in. He climbed behind the wheel, power door locks hit, bullet-proof power windows up and we took off. Deep plush seats, spacious wood-trim interior, TV, cellular phone—some life.

We followed the Long Island gold coast, then came into an isolated shoreline area. At one stretch of beach I saw a row of huge grinning rocks rooted in the water, then the beach house, or rather, mansion. It was sprawling. White and blue Georgian colonial, brick, with a lawn as big as a football field. A valet was waiting for us. He must have seen the car come up the pebbled drive—or did the ubiquitous security cameras fill him in on our arrival? I got out and Paul drove the car around, probably to a garage in the back.

The valet took me through a gleaming, pink marble floored entrance hall, down a corridor, up a plush carpeted grand staircase, and knocked on a door with ivory trim. A voice barked and the valet turned the brass door handle. I walked in.

More thick carpets, original impressionist paintings on the mahogany paneled walls, a crimson velvet divan and matching wing chairs. A sitting room? A study? It made no difference. I was ready to move in. Luxury. Thick rich luxury. I could live like this.

There was a polished Chippendale desk and behind it was King Lear himself. He got up, walked deliberately to the divan and sat down. He motioned to a club chair. I sat down.

Lloyd Henderson was dressed in an Italian silk, blue pin-striped suit. Crisp white button-down shirt, French cuffs clasped with gold cufflinks. There was no tie. He took out an envelope from his right inside jacket pocket and handed it to me. I opened it and read the contents.

It wasn't dated.

> Scandal is something we should all avoid. Keep Marilyn under control.

Fifty grand, please. You'll hear from
us again.

I put the sheet back in the envelope and gave it back to Henderson. "When did this arrive?" I asked.

"This morning."

"No idea what Marilyn was up to?"

"No idea."

"Letter and envelope was typed. Someone could have done the typing at home, or in a computer store where word-processors are on display. Or a university library. The list is endless. What do you do now? You could just pay the 50 grand and that someone might go away. On the other hand ..."

"Yes," he said. "It could be only the first payment."

"You could try a bluff. Don't pay, and see what happens."

"I hate all kinds of publicity, especially if it's scandalous Dr. Cramer," Lloyd Henderson said. "But I won't sit still for blackmail."

"What do you want me to do, Mr. Henderson?"

"You must have had experiences of this sort in your line of work."

"Not often." I was thankful for that.

"I want you to straighten this mess out, and quietly."

"Who's my client? You or your daughter?"

"I am. You deal directly with me. As for my daughter, I want her out of the picture. Marilyn gets this wildness from her. I resent my daughter, Dr. Cramer. She has always gone against my better judgment."

"Isn't there some consolation?" I said. "You have two other daughters."

"Yes. Cora and Sandra. A man couldn't wish for two more loyal daughters."

"Uh huh."

"I had hopes for Marilyn. I don't know what she could have done to instigate a blackmail threat."

I thought about the imitation painting. Maybe this type of painting was getting into the art gallery.

I would have to see Marilyn again, and I didn't want to. But it didn't look like I had any other choice. She was the only lead I had.

Did Marilyn have anything to do with forged paintings or had there been an art theft of some type?

Lloyd Henderson got to his feet. "You may as well join me for lunch, Dr. Cramer."

Lunch was in an enclosed patio in the back of the mansion. A redwood table was set for four with china and sterling. A woman in a neat blue and white uniform brought platters of prime rib, and we helped ourselves. Henderson introduced me to his two daughters, Cora and Sandra. Both were expensively dressed. Cora was 47, rather plain, with reddish brown hair. Sandra was 45, with honey blond hair and strikingly attractive facial features. After the introductions Henderson started talking about his computer and information systems business.

From the back of the porch I saw the garage, which was large enough for five cars in addition to a maintenance bay. There was a tennis court, gardens, an Olympic sized pool and, a white marble fountain.

"President Burton tells me you are an accountant—a bean counter."

"Yes, mostly managerial accounting."

"Are you a CPA then?"

"I am a Certified Public Accountant, a Certified Management Accountant, and a Certified Fraud Examiner."

Henderson waved his fork and said, "Well, you might be interested in the new computerized manufacturing system we installed in one of my plants. We're using an on-line process flow control networked with our work-in-process tracking system. We use hand-held light pens and flash-memory chips to track work-in-process through every stage of assembly,"

"A paperless system," I inserted.

"Right. It's lower cost. Paper and pencils are replaced by CRTs, keyboards, and bar code scanners. I can change the product mix at will, and we've cut investment in inventory by 50%."

"So you get assembly and test information on demand—in real time," I said.

"Correct. It gives us greater control over every phase of the operation."

"How many bar code tracking stations scan the work in process on the production line?"

"We track every single item of inventory from the time it leaves the suppliers shipping dock until the time it's sold to our customer. We scan bar codes when materials arrive in our receiving dock, when they are picked for production, at two dozen points along the production lines, and again when they are warehoused as finished products. We scan each item again when it is selected for sale to the customer."

"We give the warehouse workers a holster for their scanning guns. They consider it quite a handsome sidearm," he sniffed condescendingly, and smirked with one side of his mouth. "They fancy themselves to be high-tech cowboys."

"*Total control* is the name of the game, Mr. Cramer. I know exactly how much money I've got invested in inventories at every critical juncture—and I know exactly how much inventory is walking out the door in my employee's pockets as well. Believe me, we prosecute them to the hilt when we catch them stealing from me."

"We want materials to be delivered just-in-time for production, and we want finished products coming off the line just-in-time for sale to our customers. In this business one day can mean millions of dollars in obsolete inventory. That is something I absolutely will not tolerate from my people. I don't need to tell you, I have good people—they keep inventories at the absolute minimum," he crowed proudly.

"I read last week in a **Financial Executive** report that there will be a number of substantial changes over the next few years: widespread acceptance of electronic banking, commercial application of artificial intelligence, global connectivity, integration of corporate databases, and the ascent of the chief information officer into the executive ranks."

Barry University Library
Miami, Fla. 33161

Henderson seemed to be actually enjoying the conversation.

After the sumptuous, if heavy, meal, Paul Manfred drove me back to the train station. Not one word passed between us.

When I was got back to Grand Central, I decided to walk the 10 blocks to my accounting office. Hildy was on the phone. I waited for her to finish. "Is Tom Reardon around?"

"Yes," she said, "Want me to buzz his office?"

"Yes."

Tom walked in a few minutes later. He was a tall Irish redhead with penetrating green eyes. After graduating with a degree in accounting, he had worked for the FBI for four years investigating white-collar financial crimes.

He sat down and I said, "See if you can get a line on a Paul Manfred. He acts as a bodyguard for Lloyd Henderson, our new client. Early 20's, tall, solid build, blond hair. There's a good chance he may have a record."

"Is this okay with John?"

"Yes, we have a paying client."

I then gave him information about Marilyn and Myra Riley, the death of Teddy Noren, the maybe theft Myra had told me about, and the blackmail letter to Lloyd Henderson.

Tom went on his way, and I called Marilyn's apartment. She was there. "Are you staying there?"

"Yes," she said. "Where am I supposed to go?"

"Nowhere, I guess. I'll be right over."

"Why? I thought you were finished with me."

"No such luck." I hung up.

Five

Those who listen to the siren song of the brokers of art as an investment, should keep in mind and cast an exceedingly wary look in the direction of the salesroom commentators whose enthusiasm grows even more round-eyed as the price mounts.
—Gerald Reitlingers

I didn't expect Marilyn to be cordial and she wasn't. She lounged in a rocking chair, one leg over the other. She was wearing a loose fitting sweater and black stretch pants. Her feet were bare.

"It's your grandfather," I said, sitting down. "He received a letter today. A blackmail letter."

She was surprised, or pretended to be surprised. "What has that got to do with me?"

I repeated the contents of the letter to her, word for word. "Your grandfather asked me to look into it." I looked at her, waited for a reply.

When there wasn't any, I said, "This is no joke, Marilyn. I want you to be straight with me. What do you know about Teddy's death?"

"Nothing," she said testily.

"No forgeries of famous art works or anything like that?"

Silence.

"You'd like to help your grandfather, wouldn't you?"

Her frown soured. "Sure. Like he helped my mother. He kicked her out."

"I thought he liked you. Your mother told me he did."

"I'm his only grandchild," she said.

I said, "Why haven't Cora and Sandra ever gotten married and started families?"

"My grandfather wanted them to stay home and take care of him. I guess he's afraid of dying a miserable, lonely old man. And who'd want to marry Cora? She hasn't got a life. Sandra has potential. Or had. But she chose to stick with grandpa. I guess they're both afraid of him—or of being disinherited."

"Where were you yesterday while Teddy was doing his Dutch act?"

"Working."

"At the art gallery?"

"No. Posing."

"For whom?"

"Frank Masters. In the altogether, like auntie used to say, I'm rather popular with the artists. They like what they see."

"Why did Teddy carry a gun?"

"Maybe it made him feel more like a man," she said. "Teddy wasn't very sure of himself. He wasn't a very strong person."

Her answer was clearly evasive. I left it alone. "I'd like to talk to this Frank Masters."

"I'll give you his address. I have nothing to hide. I have every intention of cooperating with you, Mr. Cramer." Her voice now had a phony sweetness.

"This Bram Walker who does landscapes. How do I get in touch with him?"

"I'll give you his address too. Anything else you'd like to know? How about Judy Chicago? Oh, I guess you wouldn't know about her."

"I know the name."

"Oh?"

"And O'Keefe, Rivers, Gorman. I don't live in a cave, Marilyn. I've also heard of Picasso. Have you heard of Luca Pacioli?"

"Nope. Who is he? He's not renaissance."

"I smiled. Pacioli was a contemporary of Leonardo da Vinci. He was a Franciscan monk considered to be the father of accounting. He wrote a treatise about mathematics and double-entry accounting. Aren't you a bookkeeper?"

"Cute." She then smiled slightly. "I suppose I could learn to tolerate you, if you weren't so abrasive."

"Who, me? I'm the sweetest accounting Prof. in the world." I got up and stretched and took a walk through the apartment. She got up quickly and followed after me. I went into the room where I had seen the balance scales earlier. They were gone now. So was the paraffin.

Her fingers bit into my arm. Her face was a mess of anger. "What's the idea? What are you looking for?"

"Two balance scales."

She seemed to be having a hard time breathing all of a sudden. "I don't know what you're talking about."

"What kind of trouble are you in Marilyn? Are you stealing from the art gallery to pay for crack?"

She took her hand away from my arm. Her face was ghostlike. "You're crazy. You must be out of your mind. Look, you can't come in here—"

"Listen to how this sounds," I snapped. "Before you came to my office you tipped someone off. That someone came here and took the scales you were using to weigh crack cocaine. You went back and called the police. But when they arrived at the apartment, there are no scales, no crack. And you're involved with faked paintings. So fake that some blackmailer could use the information to put the bite on your grandfather—with your help or without it."

She backed away, frightened. "You can't prove it. You can't even prove there ever were any scales here. You won't go to the police. You can't afford that. You can't tell them you were here and saw two scales and didn't report a dead body to them. There's a law about failing to report a dead body. And you're a CPA. You know the law. They'll pull your license for good."

"Do you hate your grandfather that much?"

"No. I—I—" She was confused. Then she went to the divan and sat down. Her hands gripped her knees. Her knuckles were white. "I had no idea—I couldn't blackmail anyone. You don't understand."

I stood over her. "Tell me what happened. Everything. I'm listening."

She looked up at me with wet eyes. The kid could cry. She wasn't so hard-boiled deep inside.

"Teddy and I needed the money. The stuff I posed for never got into any magazines. But we never sold anything real—it was only wax. Certain dealers. They wanted crack ... and.... But I know nothing about forgeries. I'm not taking money from the gallery."

"I think I understand. Small-time cocaine dealers sometimes pass off chunks of wax as crack. The buyers can't tell the difference until someone tries to smoke it. You must not have been doing it for long. Who came here and took the scales?"

"Bram Walker."

"Why would you and Teddy need money? You both have jobs."

"Yeah, paying minimum wage. You can't live in this city on minimum wage."

"Did Teddy have any arguments with Bram Walker or Frank Masters?"

The question was beyond her. "No. Why should there be arguments? What do you mean?"

"Were you having an affair with Bram or Frank?"

"No."

I went to the painting on the easel. "Who painted this?"

"Teddy."

"Could Bram or Frank copy his style?"

"I guess so." She didn't understand my line of questioning. "Sometimes they would copy each other for fun. I don't get it. What are you saying?"

"This painting is an oil. It's a forgery. Teddy only used acrylics."

Maybe it was what I said or the way I said it—she jumped up and scrutinized the painting. "It *is* oil." She faced me, some of the cocky assurance wiped out. "What in the world is going on? You're hiding something from me." She turned suddenly on me, clenched her fists and banged them on my chest. "What is going on?" She demanded.

I grabbed her wrists, "Teddy didn't paint this forgery. It was somebody else. Why? I don't know. Teddy wasn't alone when his life was snuffed out."

That caught her. Her chest heaved and fell as she reeled in disbelief. "You think he was murdered? That's insane. Who would take the time to paint a picture?"

"I don't know. But the guy brought his own paints. Oils. And look at this, linseed oil—Teddy wouldn't have used it much. I think someone killed Teddy before or after he did the painting. He knew artists who could copy his style."

"Bram? Frank? No. You're wrong. We were all close. They were Teddy's friends. Bram did the cutting, sure. As far as I know, Frank didn't know anything about it. But Teddy knew what I was doing. But kill Teddy? There was no reason for either of them to kill Teddy."

"Maybe I'm wrong, Marilyn. I've been wrong before. But the suicide angle—it doesn't add up."

She slumped into a chair. "This is crazy." She looked up at me. "Why didn't you tell the cops?"

"Tell them my nasty suspicions? Where's the proof? A painting hastily done in oil isn't good enough. And if it was murder—how does it tie in with the blackmail angle?"

"You're the detective—uh, accountant—or whatever you are. You tell me."

"I wish I could," I said. I didn't want to alarm her, but I couldn't help but add, "Can't you see the danger you're in? Your boyfriend ends up dead, and your grandfather gets a blackmail threat. They want you to shut up. The police would love that. And the newspapers—I can just see the headlines. Your grandfather is news. Rich as Midas. Money, scandal, drugs ... and murder. The news media feed on that kind of stuff."

"What are you going to do?"

"Talk to Bram and Frank. You will help, won't you?"

She bared her teeth. "I said I would."

"Give me their addresses and phone numbers." I gave her some paper, and she wrote them on it.

"They don't have to talk to you," she pointed out. "You should take me with you."

"They'll think you turned on them."

"Who cares," she said vehemently.

Bram Walker didn't live far from Marilyn. A three story row-house, with worn granite steps leading up to the front door. It was an old building, but kept in fairly good repair. Bram Walker lived in a third floor walk-up. A girl with olive skin opened the door to us. Her eyes focused on Marilyn, and I saw the venom in her eyes.

"Is Bram in?"

"Yes," the girl said.

We walked into the room, and Marilyn introduced me to Nadja. She was tall, slim, with short black hair. She was wearing a long bath robe.

The front room was small with a plaid couch and two chairs, a bookcase full of paperbacks, a low table with a brass ashtray on it, and a book about surrealism. While she went to get Bram Walker, I picked up the book. I opened it to an illustration of a painting by Hans Arp. I flipped pages and admired some works by Rene Magritte. Could you forge paintings from pictures? Not likely.

Bram Walker strode in, bare chested. He had on short pants, with no belt. His feet were bare. He was tall and slim with dark brown hair. About 25. There was a tiny scar at the corner of his mouth. He invited us to sit down. Nadja hadn't come with him.

We all sat down, chummy like. A little hokey. Marilyn gave the introductions. Bram smiled politely.

"Mr. Cramer is an accountant," Marilyn explained. "He's working for my grandfather. He—uh—wants to ask you a few questions."

His eyebrows rose and his lips thinned. "Questions? Questions about what?"

"Teddy Noren," I said.

"Teddy? Poor chap. A good friend of mine."

"You were supposed to have lunch with him yesterday?" I said.

"Yes. In the Village. But he didn't show."

"No. Because he was dead, I'm afraid. Did you try to call him when he didn't show?"

"Oh, yes. There was no answer."

"What did you do then?"

"I went home, worked on a painting."

"Until Marilyn called you to get two balance scales and a block of wax?"

He stiffened, turned slowly to Marilyn, his face not a nice thing to see. Ugly. "Marilyn talks too much." He turned back to me and smiled. "What does an accountant have to do with this anyway? Why should I talk to you?"

"You mean you'd rather talk to the police."

Sometimes that worked, sometimes it didn't. He smiled blandly. "Do you think the police would be interested in the ravings of a lunatic, grade-B model?"

Marilyn was hurt and angry. "Bram! You have no right to say that. My grandfather is being blackmailed …"

His smile floated towards Marilyn. "I thought you didn't care for your grandfather."

"Why use the word, lunatic?" I asked. I was beginning not to care for Mr. Bram Walker. I was crossing him off my Christmas list.

"The dear child has fits of depression," he said to me. "She once had a nervous breakdown. One time at a party—"

"Never mind," I growled. "I was hoping you would cooperate. I'm not the police, but I know some police who would be very interested in your sideline."

"Like I told you—"

"I think the officer in charge would be interested in the fact you went to Teddy's apartment, killed him, did a forgery with your own paint—"

His face chalked. "Killed? Are you saying Teddy was murdered?"

"That's what I said."

"I didn't kill Teddy." He shot a glance at his long fingers. There was some paint on them. "You can't pin it on me, Mr. Cramer. Teddy was dead when I got there. Quite dead, I assure you. I thought it was suicide and I left."

"You admit you were there?"

"Yes, yes." He started to squirm. He looked at Marilyn. "I'm sorry about Teddy. Honest. He was a friend. If he was murdered, I certainly didn't do it." He looked at me. "You can't blame me for saying I wasn't there, can you? Who wants to get involved in a mess like that?"

"You're telling the truth now."

"I thought it was suicide—but murder—if I can help find his killer—well, I won't hinder you by lying. I don't really know how it helps, but I admit going there. When Teddy didn't show up for our lunch, I called him. There was no answer. So I went to his apartment. The door wasn't locked. So I went in; found him dead. It shook me up and I just left."

"Why didn't you take the scales then?" I wanted to know.

"I didn't think of it. I was scared. I couldn't think straight. Then when Marilyn called and told me I should get the scales while she was out—well, I did just that. My nerves were on edge the whole time. I pictured the police walking in and finding me there."

"You didn't bring your own paints with you?"

"No. Why should I do that?"

I told him about the oil on the easel and Teddy Noren working only with acrylic.

"How strange. I never knew him to use oils. He never knew the joys of melding texture and color." He looked at me with a grin. "I guess you wouldn't understand what I mean."

"I know enough." A stretched canvas has to be painted with a whitewash coat before the artist starts the painting. The artist usually waits for the canvas to dry before painting. But some artists don't wait for the canvas to dry. They start painting while the canvas is still wet. That way they can move the paint around in bold strokes as they use pallet knives and brushes. In case they didn't like what they had done they could change it. It's called painting wet-on-wet.

"Are you a Sunday painter?" he asked.

"I was, but I gave it all up. I did a year of sketches and drawings, and some painting. I was never very good, so I gave it up for the exciting life of an accounting professor."

"A pity. So you're a professor. They get paid more than artists. If you laid all accountants end-to-end, it'll probably be a good thing."

"I've heard that about economists and lawyers." I broke it off. "Look, I didn't come to talk about—"

He waved a hand. "All right. I was curious. I can talk endlessly about art."

"I can't. Do you have the scales here?"

"No. You can look around."

"Where did you put them?

"Sorry. I won't answer that one."

Nadja walked in. "When do we go back to work?" she said.

Bram Walker stood up. "Sorry I can't be of more help." It was a dismissal.

Marilyn and I left.

Outside, she asked, "Are you hungry?" Clearly meaning *she* was hungry.

We found a place where they served Thai food. As we ate I said, "Nadja doesn't like you very much, does she?"

"I'm more popular as a model than she is."

There was steamed rice under my intensely hot curried chicken. "Okay. Now tell me the real reason."

"She thinks I took Teddy away from her." Marilyn laughed. "Teddy never had any interest in her."

"Does Nadja stay with Bram?"

"She has to live some place," Marilyn said, as if logically. She drank some Coke. "Bram will dump her as soon as he gets tired of her."

Frank Masters lived in the Village. Bleeker Street. It was a nice apartment building with an onyx-walled lobby that had three metal benches and brass sand boxes for cigarettes near the two elevators. The was a No Smoking sign in the elevator.

The elevator took us up to the seventh floor, and we walked down the corridor on clean maroon-gray carpet. Masters opened the door for us. "Hello, Marilyn. Who is this?"

He was about 27, swarthy, with a thin mustache, and dark brown hair parted on the left side. Marilyn introduced me, and we walked into his living room. Spacious for a New York apartment.

The living room was furnished with a glass-topped cocktail table, two feet from a long white sofa, with two winged back chairs on either side of the sofa. There was a Wilton rug on the floor. Paintings covered most of the walls.

Masters was dressed casually, in open collar shirt, khaki pants, and cordovan penny-loafers. He didn't have on socks.

"I'm sorry about Teddy," he said gently to Marilyn. He looked at me with a faint smile. "And how can I help you, Mr. Cramer?"

"I'm looking into the death of Teddy Noren."

"Police?"

"No. Just a professor helping a friend. I'm working for Marilyn's grandfather."

"The wealthy Lloyd Henderson." He said it without relish. "I despise the very rich. Jealousy, I'm afraid."

"Did you pay Teddy Noren a visit yesterday?"

"No."

"You had no contact at all with him yesterday?"

"No."

"You and he were very good friends, weren't you?"

"Oh, yes. The best."

"Did he have any enemies?"

"Teddy? Mild-mannered Teddy? Of course not."

"I think Teddy was murdered, Mr. Masters."

There was no emotion in his face or voice. "I read it was suicide."

"Somebody had done an oil painting in his apartment before killing him, or after."

"Whatever for?"

"I don't know. It was a forgery."

"Strange thing to do," he mused. "I don't like discussing death. Suicide or murder. The very idea is about as unappealing as cold oatmeal."

"And you didn't see Teddy yesterday. Did you see Bram Walker?"

"Yes. We had dinner together."

"Do you know of Mr. Walker's sideline?"

He looked bored. "Sideline?"

"Crack cocaine? Imitation paintings?"

His glance at Marilyn said: you talk too much, Marilyn. "Mr. Accountant, I'm a very busy man. Work, work, work. You will forgive me, won't you?"

I was getting the brush-off. Marilyn and I stood up, and I thanked Masters for his time. Then we left.

"What now?" she said when we were on the sidewalk.

"I'm taking you home. If you get any invitations from either of the two, forget it. Stay put."

That didn't settle too well with her. "You think I'm in danger?"

"They're not exactly happy you talked to me Marilyn. And someone is selling imitation paintings."

"These aren't violent people, Mr. Cramer."

"Choir boys don't traffic in the kind of drugs you were involved with, Marilyn. And you don't know who was fronting the money for it. Beside, when you cut bags of crack with rocks made out of wax, someone is liable to get unhappy. Please use your head and listen to me."

Diluting a product with cheap materials will produce what is known as a favorable materials mix variance. However, the quality of the product may suffer if it's done to an extreme—like Marilyn's crack. That's why both favorable and unfavorable variances need to be interpreted with care. Hospitals measure patient mix, a similar concept. Some illness treatments are more profitable than others. An abnormal influx of patients requiring low-margin treatments will cause an unfavorable patient (sales) mix variance and reduce overall profitability of the hospital.

There was a taxi stand nearby with two yellow cabs waiting. We got into the first one. I gave the driver Marilyn's address. This would probably be a low margin trip for the driver—lowering his sales mix variance for the day.

"What if I get hungry?" she said.

"Have some Chinese food delivered and stay put."

Her fingers were on my wrist. "You'll call me, won't you?"

"Tonight. And tomorrow morning."

Six

Management accountants have been so involved in the details of the traditional cost accounting system that they are not aware of the 'big picture' changes that have occurred in cost structure and behavior.
—Thomas B. Lammert and Robert Ehrsam

Tom Reardon was in my sixth floor Columbia University office in Uris Hall. He was sitting peacefully, with his long legs stretched out. I stepped over his big feet and sat behind my desk.

"Paul Manfred," he said. "Did time for manslaughter. A real tough character. He got off light. Plea bargain, you know how it goes."

I gave him Frank Masters' address. Then I described Bram Walker to him. I wanted to know if someone of that description went into Masters' building lugging two laboratory scales. "That would be anytime yesterday. There's a taxi stand nearby. Talk to the cab drivers, one of them may have seen him." Then I gave him all I had on Henderson and the blackmail, the death of Teddy Noren, the Rileys, and the two sisters who stayed with their daddy.

"Paul Manfred could be in on the blackmail thing," Reardon said.

"I am not overlooking any angle. And while you're at Masters' apartment building, check to see if there's a service entrance. Mr. Walker may have gone through there with his two scales."

"Anything else, boss?"

"Yes, you need to get over to Myra Riley's art gallery. Check her account books. Is her bookkeeper, Marilyn Riley, cooking the financial records? Look for signs of money laundering. See if the cost of artwork sold is inflated. Are there any sales not supported by consignment slips—the usual routine. I doubt there's anything in the way of internal controls. But keep your eyes open for lapses in compliance with what few controls might exist."

The redheaded Irishman left and I moved to my sofa, and started going through some of my backlog of reading material. Under the seemingly endless pile of journals and technical pronouncements I found my old AICPA booklet on internal control systems. It was published back in the 1950's. But, I still keep it around, and refer to it pretty often. It's based on a largely manual accounting system for a manufacturing company. It's got great diagrams of basic paperwork flows for every major system in a business: sales and receivables, purchasing and inventory, billing and collections, payroll, *etc.* It's very useful for understanding the principles of checks and balances. I must have put it in my reading pile to pull some overheads for class.

In today's environment of electronic data interchange (EDI) where suppliers and customers exchange paperless electronic purchase orders and invoices, it never ceases to amaze me how many organizations still use old, outmoded information systems. I don't know how they keep surviving doing business that way.

Bob Kaplan at Harvard thinks they won't, especially in today's globally competitive economy. He wrote a book on the rise and fall of managerial accounting, and how outmoded accounting systems, that spread costs across products like spreading peanut butter with a blunt knife, result in inaccurate product cost determinations and uncompetitive pricing policies. He advocates a system of Activity Based Costing (ABC).

Basically, ABC says that managers should identify the specific activities that drive costs. These are known, surprisingly, as "cost-drivers." This is one of the few, truly creative labels in accounting. Accurate identification of the salient cost drivers for a product allows managers to calculate in great detail how costs will vary with the specific activities that drive production costs up or down. Once this is done, refined and detailed application of costs to products can be made based on however many cost drivers are relevant to a specific product. This gives both a more accurate product cost calculation and a more accurate basis upon which to formulate product pricing strategies.

I agree with him on that score. And with today's computing power, the cost/benefit ratio for information systems gets lower all the time, allowing more detailed cost accounting systems to be implemented at lower processing cost for most companies.

While flipping through some of the journals in the pile, I spotted in *Cost Management Systems: A Digest of the Relevant Literature*, a short review of "Pitfalls in Evaluating Risky Projects." The authors, Hodder and Riggs in the *Harvard Business Review*, argued that discounted cash flow procedures are not inherently biased against long-term investment. But managers need to set realistic hurdle rates and carefully examine their own assumptions. That's for sure.

Skimming the latest issue of *Management Accounting*, I read a piece by Ir-Woon Kim and Irjan T. Sadhwani entitled "Is Your Inventory Really All There?" They indicated that "most inventory discrepancies in manufacturing companies are due to employee, vendor, and customer errors rather than to theft." Add that to employee theft—there're errors, and then sometimes there are "errors."

Next I read a stack of newsletters: *The Art Newsletter*, *The Gray Letter*, and *The International Art Market*. In *Connoisseur*, a monthly glossy, I saw that a 19th century painting by Jean Francois Millet, called *Peasant Grafting a Tree*, sold for more than a half million. I flipped through the latest issue of *Art in America*, and fell asleep on the sofa reading *Apollo*. *Art and Action* was unopened on the floor in front of me when I awoke from a bad dream.

I dreamed I was chairing a meeting of the federal Cost Accounting Standards Board. The CASB issues accounting standards for virtually all federal government-negotiated contracts of $100,000 or more. I was addressing the learned group.

"A static budget provides cost and revenue estimates for one level of activity. Conversely, a flexible budget (also known as a dynamic budget) is prepared for more than one level of activity (*i.e.*, 13,000, 14,000, and 15,000 units of production). The reason for preparing budgets for various levels of activity is to provide managers with information about costs over a range of production activity, since the actual level may be different from the expected level."

At that moment, Glenn A. Welsch stepped out of his oil painting on the wall. He shouted, "The Just-in-Time theory of manufacturing brings raw materials and production together in such a way as to eliminate waste." Then he pulled a high powered Uzi water pistol filled with chartreuse acrylic paint out from under his suit coat and shot Charles Horngren.

As Horngren was falling to the floor mortally wounded, on his last gasp he calmly wheezed, "Cost accounting is the major obstacle for making U.S. manufacturing companies competitive. The JIT philosophy treats work-in process inventory as a liability rather than a asset. So, management cannot use a large work-in-process account as a cushion." Then in a hiss of steam Horngren dissolved into a pool of acrylic paint. What a world.

Just then Ray Garrison walked into the room. He strode to the podium where I was standing, took the microphone, and began lecturing.

"A cost is relevant to decision making only if it will change depending upon the decision. If a given cost will not change no matter what we decide, it is not relevant. A classic example is money spent in the past on mechanical repairs to a company's fleet of trucks. That cost will not change regardless of whether we decide to make another round of repairs or not. The only effect it has on the decision to incur further repair costs is in estimating the potential benefits to be gained from the new repairs. The previous repair may, or may not, interact with the new repairs in enabling the company to gain more mileage use from the truck fleet."

Just then everyone seated at the long table reached into their shirt pockets, took out little toy Matchbox trailer trucks and began racing them over the mirror-like surface of the table—crashing them into each other, and making childlike noises that sounded distinctly like, "vroom, vroom, errrrrrr ... crash!" It was truly a nightmarish scene.

To distract myself from the reversionary madness that had taken the committee members captive, I pulled my old intermediate financial accounting book out of my briefcase, turned to the end of the chapter on cash, and began working a four-column cash proof just like a numeric crossword puzzle. It was for entertainment. Something I've always found relaxing. But this time it just didn't seem to help.

Glen Welsch was quickly subsumed back into his portrait on the wall, as if drawn by a vacuum. Hmmm. Surrealistic accounting, I mused. Interesting notion. Guess that's what governments have been doing for years—like taking the S&L losses "off-budget" in order to magically reduce the federal deficit. Unreal. Guess the joke's on us. Budgeting needs to force us to take a hard, realistic look at our grandiose plans and put them in cold dollars and cents. If the numbers don't add up, whether we like it or not, it's better to adjust our plans ahead of time to something more realistic. The problem is personalities. Dominant corporate visionaries are hard to reign in without formal control procedures on the budgetary process.

Then there's gaming. Middle managers pad their budget estimates because they know top management will cut the budget, and middle managers know how much they need to operate their departments. Top management cuts the budget because they know middle managers are padding the estimates. Seems pretty silly when you think about it.

Games. Some management accounting games get nasty real fast. Like the receivables/payables game. Everyone wants to accelerate collection of their receivables and postpone payment of their payables. Great way to off-load your debt onto the other guy's balance sheet—just drag out your account payments, and he'll be forced to lean on his lines of credit to cover the cash shortage. If you're big enough, and he's small enough, he'll pile on enough debt financing to put himself in trouble. Then enter a "friend." He approaches the little guy and offers to buy out his financially distressed company— at a steep discount, of course. If the mark sells out, the friend turns around and resells the company to the big outfit. They just scooped it from the little guy for a song.

I helped a small businessman once who saw it coming. His biggest customer was up to owing him $4,000,000. But he knew his own limits, and wasn't about to be bullied by anyone. Losing their account wasn't as serious as losing his whole company. So he got tough with them. "Pay the account or I'll shut you off." He threatened—and he meant it. They puffed back, "You don't shut us off. Nobody shuts us off. You shut us off and you'll never do business with us again." After all, they were one of the biggest retailers in the industry—and his biggest customer. He said, "Watch me."

He shut them off—cut off all shipments of his product. They paid the $4,000,000. Why? He was supplying a quality product they were making money on reselling. They didn't want to lose him as a supplier. And he won their respect as a tough businessman. We had done a cash flow analysis and figured he could risk losing the $4,000,000. It would have hurt, but he could have absorbed it. A big customer like that who doesn't pay isn't a good customer, no matter how much product they order. Funny we don't teach more on this in B-schools. Might help save our students $4,000,000 some day.

Then there's sheer politics. Like the government clerk who keeps putting a contractor's payment vouchers on the bottom of his in-basket pile, until the payee takes him out to lunch and remembers the clerk's birthday with an envelope full of cash. It's amazing how fast government paperwork seems to get processed by that kind of jerk.

I floated in my dream to a ritzy restaurant lounge scene in Baltimore. There he was, small-time state government engineer in one of his $1,200 custom tailored black silk Brooks Brothers suits—half stewed. "Lenny," his alcohol reeking breath exuded rancid oil. "Why don't you smarten up, and join with us?" He ran his fingers disdainfully up and down my gray department store suit coat lapel. "Then you could be wearing suits like mine."

"I like my suits just fine." I shot back. Sniveling wretch. Would sell his own grandmother for a lousy chance to shakedown another small-time city contractor.

Government contractors. That's what the CASB is about. Can't let contractors dump all their unrelated, underapplied overhead onto their cost-plus government contracts. The ones where companies are reimbursed for their production costs plus a predefined profit. Under the government's cost-plus contracting system, government contractors have an economic incentive to increase costs of production since they will be reimbursed—*i.e.*, add employees to the payroll, spare no expense on production, and lavish perquisites on managers and customers. More subtle manipulations also occur when costs associated with production unrelated to a government contract are shifted to the government contract for reimbursement through overhead allocation methods.

For example, the costs of building a stealth bomber might be primarily driven by direct engineering hours since the product is new and unique. On the other hand, the costs of building a commercial jetliner might be primarily driven by direct labor hours, since the engineering problems and designs are better understood and more standardized. Therefore, by using direct engineering hours as an allocation basis for applying overhead to the two separate contracts, a disproportionately large amount of overhead will be assigned to the stealth bomber—and will be reimbursed by the defense agency. The commercial jetliner will be charged with less overhead, and will therefore provide a more profitable sale to an airline. So, the government will be unwittingly subsidizing the costs and profitability of commercial production activities.

That's a main reason why the CASB devoted a lot of attention to overhead allocation rules. Then they got defunded by Congress in September 1980. Four years later the Federal Acquisition Regulations (FAR) became effective and codified the CASB rules. CASB was refunded back in

1988. Now their rules extend beyond just the original domain of defense contracts, to all types of federal government contracts.

The lounge waffled and began to fade; someone was walking toward me.

As I became fully awake, the department secretary was approaching my office. "There's a lady outside. Myra Riley."

"Escort the lady into my parlor." I said groggily.

Myra Riley had on a knit pink dress with flowers on it.

"I thought I would hear from you." As my thoughts began to clear, I brought her up to date on the blackmail threat.

"You think it's because of the theft?" she said.

"Marilyn denies any such thing."

"I'm so confused ..."

"Aren't we all?"

"I'm glad my father kept you on."

"Oh, I'll muddle my way through." Then I told her why I thought Teddy was murdered. That shook her a bit. She wanted to know if I thought Marilyn was involved in that. I told her I didn't think so.

"There were two balance scales in Marilyn's apartment. There was a forged painting. I saw them when I found Teddy's body. While your daughter was in my office, the scales disappeared."

"But—"

"You're a big girl, Myra. I think Marilyn did her dealing out of her own apartment."

"Dealing?"

"Crack cocaine, Myra. Or actually simulated crack, so she says—she was passing off chunks of paraffin as the real thing. A pretty hazardous practice, I'm sorry to say. Maybe also some imitations of famous paintings."

That shook her more than the realization Teddy may have been murdered. "I think Marilyn's aboveboard at this point. She's feeling mortified, and pretty scared. She introduced me to two of Teddy's buddies and they weren't happy about her talking to me. One of them, Bram Walker, made the scales disappear. The other one, Frank Masters, may also be involved."

"You think they're blackmailing my father?"

"They have the leverage," I said.

"You'll stop them, won't you?" She reached across my desk and touched my hand, her eyes pleading.

"That's what they're paying me for."

"Marilyn was without a father for too many years," she said. Her fingernails were digging into my hand. "And I was without a husband. It's bad, Mr. Cramer."

We went outside. The air was cool, even if smelling like grime and the ceaseless carbon monoxide. "Shall I drop you off?" I said, waving at a cab.

"If you have other plans ..."

"I'm a working professor don't forget."

The cab stopped for us. I opened the door for her and we got in. I slammed the door and gave the driver her address. She sat by the far door and stared wistfully at me.

"Do you work 24 hours a day?" she asked from the blurry darkness.

"I'm a night bird."

She was silent after that. It started to drizzle. Urban rain. April was like that. When we got to her place the temperature had lowered. Myra got out and I watched her go up the stairs to her apartment.

I stopped at my apartment to check the mail, and then proceeded to my accounting office. Tom was already there. "No cabby saw Walker go into Masters' apartment building," he reported. "And there is a service entrance. Want me to take a look at Masters' apartment?"

"I can't ask you to do that. Don't get caught."

"Who, me?"

"While you're in there, look for pipes, scales, chunks of wax—any signs of a small-time crack cutting operation. Check to see if there are any forged paintings."

"Do I take anything away?"

"No. I don't want Masters to know anyone's been there. He probably won't keep any incriminating stuff in his apartment anyway. And don't forget to check the financial records at the art gallery."

"I'll give the place a good shakedown, don't worry." Tom went away and I got hold of Hildy. "Would you get me some coffee and sweets, Hildy. Maybe a Danish."

"You'll get fat."

"A cheese danish."

"I'll order something for myself." She said perkily. "Your treat. You've been here more this week than you're normally here in a month."

"The president of Columbia is making me do this. I should be on the computer doing research. Oh, well, he's the boss."

Grant sent for me and I gave him a rundown. He didn't look too well. Unusually deep circles under his eyes—down into his cheeks. "I hate blackmailers. I didn't get much sleep last night. I'll have to taper off," I reported.

"Look, play this guy Henderson along. There's millions there."

"Millions and millions," I said, disgusted with him. "That's what my president said." I went to my small desk and ate my cheese danish and drank my regular acidic coffee. I only wanted to teach and do research.

Research. When would I ever learn to budget my time to factor in more research. It's no different than budgeting for a business. Failing to meet cash budget requirements can lead to dilemmas like one computer leasing company experienced when the president discovered he could either meet the payroll, or meet the bond payments—but there was not enough cash available to meet both. Sort of like when I can work on forensic accounting cases like this one, or write and publish a technical research paper, but can't do them both at once.

That company president's fiduciary responsibility required that the payroll be met first, which left no choice but to default on the bonds. The company had to declare bankruptcy. But, fortunately, the president was able to find a larger company willing to buy out the creditors and keep the company operating. To someone responsible for running a multimillion dollar, publicly traded company, that kind of stress can be pretty significant. For a junior professor, the stress of failing to publish is similarly heavy. But of course, being tenured, I mostly need to publish for raises, promotions, and favorable teaching schedules. It also helps bring new material into my classroom lectures, as does my forensic accounting work.

Tom called. "I'm calling from Masters' place," he said. "No balance scales. But there's a paint mixer. Can I keep it?"

"No."

"No pretty white powder, or waxy-looking rocks? No forgeries?"

"No. Masters walked out with some woman so I let myself into his apartment. Went through the service entrance. Piece of cake. Can't stay long 'cause I don't know when they'll be back."

"What did this woman look like?"

He described Nadja.

"She's Walker's model," I told Tom. "Probably models for Masters too. Better get out of there."

"Will do." He hung up.

I waited for Tom in the lobby, and we went for dinner. The rain had stopped during the night and the streets looked almost clean. We ordered sandwiches and soft drinks at a nearby deli.

I told Tom about Grant wanting me to play Henderson along. Tom shook his head in disgust. "That bum," he said. "He's got enough dough. Why does he have to be so greedy?"

"Maybe he wants to be in Henderson's class."

"No way," Tom grinned. "I've read about Lloyd Henderson. He makes more money than some of those Hollywood directors."

"Myra hinted last night that there's something between her sister, Sandra, and Paul Manfred—they could be behind the blackmail threat."

"She's old enough to be his mother," Tom snorted.

"Don't tell me you've never heard of older women going out with younger men. Sandra's in that big mansion with no one to play games with but Paul Manfred. Stranger things than that have happened."

"Would she set up her own father for a play like that?"

I shrugged. "She doesn't have the money, according to Myra. So she may want to make sure she has some for herself. And kow-towing to the old man all the time may have left her bitter towards him."

"Look, let's say that's the play. Sandra and Paul against Henderson. Okay. But why 50 grand? That's small potatoes for a guy like Henderson. It doesn't ring true."

Tom had something there. "It does seem odd. But if 50 grand is the first payoff with more to follow ..."

"Sooner or later the old man would be bound to catch on to who's squeezing him if he has to continue payments."

We continued eating. The whole thing seemed out of kilter. And where did Teddy's death come into the scene?

It was getting chilly when we walked along the crowded sidewalk back to the office, but not cold enough to warrant overcoats. We sat in the office and discussed the death of Teddy Noren.

"You really think he was murdered?" Tom asked.

"An auditor's intuition," I said.

"Then he would have known about the blackmail?" Tom asked.

"Maybe. What about the forgery business? He could have been ready to set the police on whoever was—"

Tom shook his head. "No! If his girl was in on it, then he knew about it and was part of the play."

"We're going around in circles."

Hildy walked in and sat on the desk. "What are you gossips gabbing about?"

I told her.

"I think I have the answer to the 50 thousand dollar question," Hildy said, almost taunting.

"Let's hear it." I was interested. Hildy was one sharp cookie.

"Simple," she said. "To see if he'll bite."

I thought I knew what she meant. "Explain," I said.

"If he pays up, then the blackmailer will figure he really has Henderson hooked. He'll keep asking for more or ask for one big lump sum. On the other hand, if Henderson fights back, well, the blackmailer may just back off, figuring it isn't worth the effort."

"Henderson won't take the chance of not fighting back," I said. "He'll pay one and then fight like a tiger. He's not the type to let anyone bleed him dry."

"You don't know," Hildy said. "Grandfathers can be tenaciously protective of their grandchildren, even more so than their own kids."

I had a feeling we weren't even close to what was really going on. We were dancing along the edges, skirting the periphery, not even close to the heart of the matter.

Teddy's murder, forgery, artists, models, and blackmail. A lot of puzzle pieces, but put them all together and what did we get? Nothing. It was jumbled up. A mess. It just didn't all fit.

I finally chased them out and got on the phone. I called Marilyn Riley. She wasn't in. I tried Myra. "I was going to call you," she said, "but—"

"Foolish pride?"

"Don't be silly. You might think I was chasing you."

"That's ridiculous. Have you heard anything from Marilyn?"

"Yes. This afternoon. She stopped over and borrowed some money. I think she should get out of that apartment. But she doesn't have the money."

"Did she say where she was going?"

"Some shopping."

"I think Marilyn should move in and stay with you," I said. "Just for a few days."

"She'll crowd my kitchen."

"She's your daughter, not mine."

"I'll suggest it," Myra said coolly.

"How about dinner tonight to try to solve this puzzle?"

"Okay, there's a nice place on Most Street," she said. "I feel like Chinese tonight."

"Is seven okay? I'll pick you up."

"That'll be fine." She hung up.

I did some more thinking but got nowhere. The mess was still a tangled mess.

Too many fragments and they didn't seem to fit together. There has to be a flaw somewhere. How do I find it? This puzzle was a lot like trying to solve standard cost variance problems. When you're trying to determine overhead variances there's several different ways to slice the data. There's one-way, two-way and three-way analysis of overhead variances. The three-way method usually separates variable cost overhead variance items from the fixed cost overhead variance items. Thus, three-way analysis actually doubles to make six-way analysis. But, by construction, two of the variances (the variable overhead volume variance and the fixed overhead efficiency variance) will always equal zero. Therefore, three-way analysis doubles to six-way, less two that are always zero, leaving four-way—but we still call it three-way. But I have seen some books that refer to four-way analysis of overhead variances. Guess it just keeps the students guessing.

I called Lloyd Henderson's office. Mr. Henderson was too busy to talk to anyone, I was told. I insisted my name be given to him. He finally got on the line. "Hear anything from our invisible friend?" I asked.

"No, Dr. Cramer." His voice was raspy. "If I had, I would have called you." There was a sharp click and I was alone in the world with the rest of the disconnected undesirables.

I thought some unkind things about my paying client, put on my coat and told Hildy I would see her tomorrow. Maybe I'd put in a full day's work.

On the way home, a man started following me and stayed after me for two solid hours. He was short and his hair was the color of ginger. Young, stocky, in a blue serge suit. I let him follow me so that I could memorize him in my mind. When the picture was complete I played mind games with him. He had a partner, a man in a late model car. The shadow wasn't too good because he stayed across the street instead of staying behind me. Could be he wanted me to know I was being tailed. Some auditors learn to take a different route home every night.

When it was time to lose him I did. He and his partner. By that time I had the plate number of the car.

Hildy was still in the office, so I called her from a phone booth and gave her the number. Then I went to the art gallery. None of the paintings in the small shop or in inventory appeared to be noticeable fakes. Then I went home. In the Jacuzzi I relaxed with a cold Pepsi. Caffeine. Having this whirlpool tub installed was one of the best decisions I ever made—it's one thing about home I really enjoy. So, there was no connection between the art gallery and the fake paintings—at least not for the time being.

Myra was dressed in a teal-green, finely embroidered silk dress with a small beaded jacket and had a jade pendant on a slender gold chain around her neck. She looked elegantly beautiful. A taxi took us to Chinatown.

I had been in this restaurant before. Everything was good except the won-ton soup. Someone boiled water and dragged a chicken feather through it. But the hard-boiled quail eggs wrapped in bacon—a sumptuous favorite.

"Did you talk to Marilyn?" I said, munching on luscious General Tso's chicken.

"She says she thinks you're wrong and that she's not in any real danger, but she did agree to stay the night at my place. She dropped in for my keys."

She tasted my pungent chicken, and I tasted her shrimp in rich brown lobster sauce.

When we left it was dark and the street was crowded. It took about five tries to get a taxi.

Seven

So the way to express the goal is this? Increase throughput while simultaneously reducing both inventory and operating expense.
—Eliyahu M. Goldratt and Jeff Cox

An hour later I was asleep. Out cold. I had no nightmares.

It was going to be a cool day. But no drizzle. I had breakfast, and a subway took me to the 116th street and Broadway stop. When I came up out of the station, I found myself directly in front of the massive gates of Columbia University.

The surrounding neighborhood is somewhat dangerous, bordering on the Harlem section of New York. Once on campus, however, there is no sense of danger. It is a beautifully treed campus with a large central lawn and majestic pillared buildings.

Once in the center of the campus, I made a left turn and headed toward Uris Hall, where the Business School is located. The walk is pleasant, with trees on both sides of a nicely maintained brick walk.

There was a memo on my desk. Call Henderson. I had to find a large uninterrupted block of time to prepare for my upcoming expert witness testimony. But when?

"A letter arrived this morning," Henderson said. "I'm staying home today. My staff will take care of business. When can I expect you?"

"Sometime this afternoon."

"That will be all right. Paul will meet your train."

I called Grant's office. He had already spoken to Henderson. "Henderson's man wants you to deliver the money personally."

"He could have sent the money and the instructions by messenger. I'm merely a professor."

"Maybe he has something to confide in you," Grant said. "What's the difference? You have to cater to your clients. The customer is always right. We'll teach you how to be a real forensic accountant. Maybe someday you can write a novel and get tenure."

"I already have tenure. Besides, novels don't count. Only technical research articles. Remember the famous book *Love Story*. It's author was denied tenure at Harvard."

Next I called Hildy. "I called in that license plate number yesterday."

"The number belongs to Dutch Selgado," Hildy said.

Where does Dutch Selgado fit into this mess?

"Dutch is an underworld figure, with a finger in several pies. Pies bubbling over with loan sharking, numbers, extortion, and drugs. He's been in the papers numerous times, sometimes smiling with his arm around some tabloid starlet, and sometimes smiling standing next to a jockey or race-horse trainer. He is about 55, balding, with bulbous eyes. Good luck!"

When I got to Long Beach, it wasn't Paul Manfred who met me. Her name was Sandra Henderson and she was Henderson's daughter, and we had met once during lunch at his mansion. She was behind the wheel of a silver colored Porche 944, with a scarf around her head, dressed in black stretch slacks and madras shirt. She opened the passenger side door, and I got in the car.

"Where's Paul?" I asked.

"I told him I would pick you up." She grinned at me and stepped on the accelerator. "I'm better company than Paul, aren't I? He's sour. Dull."

"And you're happy as a lark, is that it?"

"I'm happy when I feel like being happy. Today I feel like being happy. You missed lunch."

"I'll make up for it."

"How about dinner tonight?"

"You're my client's daughter. How would it look?"

"Don't worry about my father. I admit my father can be rather truculent when he wants to be, but I can handle him."

"I thought it was the other way around," I said.

She looked sharply at me.

A car was coming towards us, and she swerved hard, missing the other vehicle by inches. Then she laughed. Recklessly. "Look, Lenny, do I have to drag you off to dinner by the heels?"

"No, you don't have to go that far."

"I admit my sister and I have been under my father's heel for a long time. But I'm wriggling out, slowly, surely. Cora wants to stay exactly the way she is. That's her business," she added icily.

"But your father holds the purse strings," I reminded her.

"Yes," she said seriously. "There's always that. Money. You can't do much without money. But my time—" She stopped abruptly, thinking, perhaps she was talking too much? "Don't worry about little Sandra. Sandra is finally growing up. Sandra will find a way."

"With Paul?"

Her face turned ugly. She glanced at me. "Who's been talking to you? That little vampire Myra?"

"No," I said. "It stands to reason, doesn't it? Paul is a young guy, good-looking, and there's not much else to chose from in that big mansion of yours."

She faced the road and didn't say anything. That hit a nerve ... something I wasn't supposed to know. She and Paul. So they were seeing each other. So what? Why should she mind my knowing? Unless there was more to it than that.

She braked the car in front of the house, and we got out.

We walked up the flagstone front-walk to the door and she took me to the entrance to her father's study. "I'll be out back," she said. "See me before you leave. Look, I'll drive you to the station, okay?"

"Sure." I opened the massive study door and went inside.

Mr. Henderson came directly to the point. "I've received instructions. Here they are. And here is 50 thousand dollars, in 50's. You will deliver the money tonight. My first, and last, payment."

I read the letter. There was nothing in it except the instructions. I put the letter and the money away. The money was in a brown expanding folder, taped down with the kind of packing tape you get in the post office. Mr. Henderson didn't look happy. I didn't feel happy.

"Who else knows about this?" I asked.

"No one. Have you made any progress?"

"No," I said.

"You're not doing such a great job, are you? No matter. Since you're a bean counter, maybe you can help me with a report. I have an income statement prepared by the CFO of one of my companies, under the direct costing method. How does it differ from the normal approach?"

"Absorption approach."

"What?"

"The normal way is called the absorption approach. Direct costing—often called variable costing—is computed differently.

"How?"

"Well, absorption costing inventories total material, labor, variable overhead, and *fixed* overhead costs. This method is used to value inventory and calculate cost of goods sold for *external* financial reports. It's required for taxes. It can also be used for product pricing decisions based on the full cost of production."

I stopped for a tense moment, looked Henderson straight in the eye and continued steadily. "With variable costing, *fixed* factory overhead is not charged to the cost of units produced—say computers. Instead fixed factory overhead is charged to expense in the time period in which it is incurred. It does not become a part of the inventoried cost of the products."

"In other words, this fixed factory overhead is deducted directly from sales just like sales salaries and administrative costs."

"Exactly," I said.

"So what's the advantage of using this variable costing approach?"

"It's better for internal decision making. It doesn't allow period costs—like straight line depreciation on your factory building—to be shifted across time periods as inventory levels change."

"What do you mean?"

"When fixed overhead costs are charged to a unit of product, they sit on the balance sheet in the asset account, Inventory. The fixed overhead doesn't get expensed right away. That's how absorption costing works. If the inventory piles up, and the items aren't sold until the next time period, that straight line depreciation is also shifted into the second time period. It gets expensed in the income statement as part of cost of goods sold only when the unit is sold—not in the time period when the cost was incurred."

"Anyone who has ever done taxes for a manufacturing firm knows the importance of ending inventory in determining deductible costs of goods sold. The higher the ending inventory cost valuation, the lower the deductible cost of goods sold, and the higher the taxable income. That's one reason why the IRS requires absorption costing—to increase tax revenues over the short run. They even have a whole section called the Uniform Capitalization Rules under Internal Revenue Code (IRC) Section 263A specifically defining what costs *must* be capitalized into the asset account, Inventory."

"Direct costing is the theoretically superior approach because it doesn't allow the shifting of fixed costs across time periods just by manipulating inventory levels. I read an article once, called, "How to Handle Manufacturers' and Processors' Inventories at Cost," in **Tax Ideas**. It gives a solid illustration of applying the Section 263A rules. Worth looking at."

"The Institute of Management Accountants (formerly the National Association of Accountants) has given seven examples for improved decision making. I'll send you a copy of their report. *Variable* manufacturing cost represents an inventory costing approach which corresponds more closely with the *current* cash outlays necessary to manufacture products." I sounded suspiciously like a professor in front of a classroom.

I abruptly changed the subject. "Do you have a copy of the serial numbers on these bills?"

"No. I want him paid off and out of my life. I don't want him caught so he could babble a lot of slanderous nonsense to the police and the newspapers."

I left the study and went outside to find Sandra. She was sitting on a white bentwood rocker on the back porch, sipping something green out of a longstem crystal glass. She had changed into a cotton summer dress with a square neckline and short sleeves. I sat down, and she asked if I wanted something to drink. I said no.

"What's Paul to you?" I asked.

"Someone to talk to. That's all."

I didn't believe her. "What's he to your father?"

"A bodyguard."

"That's all?"

"Call him a troubleshooter if you want."

"I want."

"I told my father not to expect me for dinner," she said. "Now you'll have to take me out."

I wanted to say something witty, but I couldn't think of anything to say. So I grunted. Sometimes I'm good at grunting.

She finished her frothy drink and drove me to the train station. She called the house from the station and told someone to pick the car up. When the train arrived we climbed on and settled down in an unusually quiet car.

"What do you think of my father?" she said.

"Another powerful business man."

"He hates to spend a dime," she said. "And he has so many. There'll be more dimes when he puts a patent on a new invention he's got going. A faster, more powerful computer microchip. Smaller than anything. My father is a shrewd man, ruthless. His only love is his paintings. He's been collecting them for years."

Paintings? Teddy, Frank and Bram were painters. Myra owned an art gallery and Marilyn worked there. Was there a connection?

"What kind of paintings?"

She shrugged her shoulders. "The good artists. The expensive ones. Picasso, Turner, Winslow—"

"Are you kidding?"

"No. Why?"

"I hope they're well guarded."

She laughed. "Who was it? Edward G. Robinson once said that a person doesn't collect paintings—paintings collect the person. They're all safe. In a special room. With trip alarms, like the McGuffey."

"I should hope so."

"Now let's talk about us."

We walked from Grand Central Station to an outside subway entrance. I hate the New York subways. Dirty, smelly, crime ridden. Like rats underground. They find a dead body in the tunnels about once a day, it seems. We went on to my apartment. I made her a cup of hot chocolate, went into my bedroom, shucked off my clothes, put on a terry cloth bathrobe. She was busy listening to classical CD's when I walked to the bathroom, shaved and showered. I put on my bathrobe, went back into my bedroom and put on fresh clothes. I had left the money and the directions on my dresser at a certain angle, with a single hair carefully placed on top of them. Both items had been moved and the hair was gone. I knew Sandra had picked them up and read the directions. What could she gain by that? Was the information for her or for Paul?

The phone rang before we left. It was Myra. I talked to her without mentioning her name. I told her I couldn't see her tonight, that I was working.

"Do I have a rival?" Sandra asked when we went downstairs.

"We're just going for dinner," I told her sternly. "No airs. Just dinner. Then you're going home."

"I don't like being rejected," she said tightly.

"We've just met," I said. "You'll have to grow on me."

We ate and then went back to Grand Central for the train. We said good-by, and I went to deliver the goods.

It was dark and the city was seething with vulgar life. From Grand Central, on 42nd Street, to Sixth Avenue there weren't too many people, but then, as if guillotined, they were out in full force. The prostitutes, the pimps, the addicts, the pushers, and the thrill-seekers were everywhere. It was a crowded, bizarre menagerie on Times Square, with all the classes mixing. The innocent, getting snared by temptation, brushing shoulders with the ones who lived under it from day to day.

Almost lost amidst this Times Square jungle I saw a small storefront jammed between two crummy joints. It had a small neon sign in the front window reading, "Jesus Saves." The young woman standing out front was handing out something. What was she doing here? It was as if her face was radiant. She actually had love for the urchins existing on this sordid bottom rung of humanity. They never ceased to amaze me ... they had something I didn't. She walked up to me and handed me a blue leaflet. It was a small Gospel leaflet. I glanced at it, thanked her, and slipped it into my shirt pocket.

I kept on to Eighth Avenue, turned right, walked up past the honky tonks and dives. Outside a sleazy lounge called Ned's I stopped to look at my watch. It was the right time.

"Hi, pal."

I looked down at a dwarf. He had craggy features, and he wore a seedy leather jacket.

He looked up at me, happy as a kid with an ice cream cone. He was about 40, and his oily hair was black. A hunk of it fell over his pimply forehead.

"Got the packet?" he said.

"What's the password?"

"What?"

"Password." I smiled and handed it over.

It started to drizzle again. Crazy month, April. He stowed the 50 grand under his jacket, turned and whistled his way away.

That was it. I had delivered the money. No mishaps.

I went home.

Outside my door I fished for my keys. Then they appeared as if by magic ... the guy who had done some tailing and a man with bulbous eyes.

Dutch Selgado.

"Don't mind us," Dutch said. "Just go right in, pal. There won't be any trouble."

The other man had a hand in his jacket pocket. I didn't have a gun on me. Don't like having to carry one anyway. Well, a clear head will have to do for now. I wasn't in a position to have gone for a gun anyway. They'd caught me blind-sided. I would have been shot dead in my tracks.

So I opened the door and went in, followed by Dutch Selgado and his friend.

I switched on the lights and sat down. The two took chairs. Dutch said, "You know me?"

"Yes," I said.

He was 55 if he was a day. There was menace in his oily voice.

"No, you don't, pal."

Who was I to argue? "Okay. I don't."

Dutch grinned at his companion. "You see? A smart baby. A very smart baby."

The other man grunted.

Dutch reached inside his jacket and came out with the folder that I had given the dwarf. These boys made good time. It had been opened. He tossed it to me. I caught it. "Count it."

I counted. Fifty grand. I tossed it back. "So?"

"So nothing, pal," Dutch said. "You delivered and you didn't take. I always expect the worst in people. How would you like to keep this dough?"

I got to my feet and the companion whipped out a gun. "I need a drink of water," I said.

"Stow it," Dutch grumbled. His friend put the pearl handled, stainless steel .380 semiautomatic away, and I poured myself some iced tea. I sat down again.

"You did hear what I said, didn't you?" Dutch said. He took a cheap cigar from a breast pocket, clipped it with a cigar cutter and stuck the thing in his mouth.

"Yeah. I heard." I drank as Dutch lit his cigar. "What's the catch?"

"The idea is," Dutch said, "you wait till I give you orders, and then you do exactly what I say."

"I'm not my own boss, Dutch."

He grinned at me. "I know. And you also know who I am, and you can call me Dutch. But nobody is to know I was here talkin' to you—that's our little secret. Now Henry here, is one guy I can count on. If I tell Henry to break your legs, he'll do it. If I tell him to plant you in a field where nobody will ever find you, he'll do it. I would hate to have to deprive your students of your wonderful lectures. Catch on?"

I told him I caught on.

"I want you on tap for something," Dutch said. "Fifty grand is a lot of dough."

"Why me?"

"Because you're in it. You've been suckered, pal. You can have this dough right now. You see, pal? I trust you. Don't I, Henry? Do you want the dough now?"

"I have a client. I have a boss."

"Don't be stupid," he barked. "Or is this some kind of act?" His face was dark with menace. "I come here in good faith. I offer you 50 grand. And you give me lines. I don't like it. Understand?" He demanded. "Are you in or out?" he demanded.

"You haven't told me what this is all about." Sure, I was stalling. Not for time. For information.

Dutch sighed. "You'll know when the time comes."

"I'll have to think about it."

Henry had his gun out again. "Let me 'explain' it to him, boss. That'll make his mind up."

I was beginning to dislike Henry. I looked at Dutch. "It would be nice if I knew what I was getting myself into."

Dutch stood up. Henry stood up.

"Put the gun away," Dutch said. Henry did what he was told. But he wasn't happy about it. His little power moment was being spoiled.

Bulbous eyes marauded over my face. "Twenty-four hours, pal. That's all you get. You'll give me an answer by then." He left, followed by helpful Henry.

I locked the door and made myself another cold drink. Wasn't feeling too well. I didn't like being threatened with guns, but then again, who did?

I looked out the window but didn't see anyone loitering around. It was still drizzling. I changed into my pale blue pajamas, and got into bed. Before going to sleep, I picked up the little Gospel leaflet I had gotten from the girl in Times Square. I looked it over and read it through. It made sense. I switched off the light, and drifted into a surprisingly restful sleep.

Eight

> *Under a job order cost system, the three basic elements of cost—direct materials, direct labor, and factory overhead—are accumulated according to assigned job numbers. The unit cost for each job is obtained by dividing the total units for the job into the job's total cost. A cost sheet is used to summarize the applicable job costs.*
> —R.S. Polimeni, F.J. Fabozzi and A.H. Adelberg

I got to the accounting office early, and when Tom came in I had him join me. He listened as I told him about my delivering the money to the dwarf and the later visit by Dutch and Henry.

"Twenty-four hours?"

"I have just that," I said. "Twenty-four hours to make up my mind."

Tom was amused. "What are you going to do?"

"Start packing."

"I'd better stick to you like glue."

"I would appreciate that. I would also appreciate a whole regiment. That Henry looks trigger happy."

"But where does Dutch fit into the scheme of things?"

I shrugged my shoulders. "Don't know. But that 50 grand was a test. Somebody is after bigger game."

"Like what?"

"Don't ask me. Maybe more money. A heck of a lot more money."

"So with Henderson forking over the 50 grand, Dutch knows he's a pushover?"

"That's the best theory so far," I said. "Unless Dutch is muscling in on someone's racket."

Hildy walked in.

We told everything to Hildy with the understanding that it wasn't to be repeated to John Grant. Grant liked things uncomplicated. And he wouldn't relish the thought that someone had the idea one of his partners could be bought for 50 grand, even under duress.

I would tell Grant what I felt he needed to know and no more.

Later, Tom and I went down for lunch. He asked me why I didn't take the bribe money.

I pretended shock. "I'm honest. I'm a CPA, among other things."

"Fifty grand is 50 grand," Tom said firmly. "Take the dough and run." He munched on bread and meat. "What could Dutch do, go to the police?"

I drank some of my drink. "He could send Henry after me."

Tom dismissed Henry with a wave of his hand. "A thug. Take away that gun and what have you got? A spineless punk."

"I have no intentions of testing that hypothesis. Punks or no punks."

"No 50 grand?"

"No 50 grand," I echoed.

"Then I suggest you take one of the .45's from the office. We have several, and all in excellent condition."

"I'm not a very good shot. Out at the practice range, what I lack in accuracy I make up for by being inconsistent."

"I'll stick with you then," Tom said. By the way, I looked over the financial records at the art gallery. Everything seems okay. I didn't spot any signs of embezzlement. No revenues unsupported by purchase invoices or consignment slips—unless, of course, what I found were fakes. Its a small business. They could be selling anything. But guess who has loaned the gallery money? Your friend Dutch Selgado. $120,000."

"Has any of the loan been paid back?"

"Yes. The original loan was for $520,000. So $400,000 has been paid back. What do you think?"

"Was there evidence of a cash influx at the time the loan was booked?"

"Good question," Tom replied. "I couldn't find any. I'll have to check some more though. There's a huge amount of paintings on consignment. Try this on for a minute: Dutch fronts the gallery cocaine, rather than cash. Maybe the offsetting debit is to Paintings Inventory or something—I need to check more. In any event, the gallery then sells the drugs, takes a cut, and funnels the rest of the cash back to Dutch in the form of loan repayments. A slick way to launder drug money," Tom smiled cynically.

"When you go back, try to determine if fake paintings are being sold to just a few customers at inflated values."

"Good idea," Tom responded. "Oh, here is a list of some of the art work sold by the gallery during the past year. Maybe you can better determine if they're being sold at fair market values."

I put the list into my briefcase, and snapped it closed. I thought about my predicament. I'm a CMA—Certified Management Accountant—maybe in this situation it stood for Certified Maniac Association. Of course, a CMA was a certificate from the Institute of Management Accountants (IMA), formerly the National Association of Accountants. They have an important ethics code. There are more than 11,000 CMAs nationally now.

I also have my CPA certificate—Certified Public Accountant. The CPA exam is offered by the American Institute of CPAs, with more than 300,000 members who are auditors and financial advisors. The 95,000 member IMA is composed of accountants who work for companies. With public accounting growing less dramatically than management accounting, both organizations are vying to dominate the field of management accounting.

The body of knowledge tested in the CMA exam is broader than the CPA exam. The CMA exam covers economics and finance, information systems, organizational behavior and ethics, quantitative methods, and internal and external reporting—with heavy emphasis on cost and managerial accounting.

The five-part CMA exam is not 60% multiple choice like the CPA exam. The CMA exam has a heavy emphasis on essay and analytic problem solving. I can still remember studying from Irv Gleim's *CMA Examination Review* manual.

The difference between a CPA and a CMA is analogous to the umpire and pitcher in a baseball game. A CPA is similar to the umpire in that he or she makes sure that the appropriate external reporting rules are followed. Conversely, the CMA is like a pitcher trying to win the game (*i.e.*, execute the best strategy to beat the competition).

About four out of every five accounting graduates obtain entry-level positions in business, government, and education. Less than 30% initially go into public accounting, and many of those move to industry in less than 10 years. So the vast majority of accountants end up working in managerial accounting roles over the long run.

Then there's the Association of Certified Fraud Examiners—CFEs. For those who prefer the exciting life. With all of the Savings and Loan failures, real estate bankruptcies, and insurance company failures, litigation support and expert testimony—this forensic accounting game—has become a service growth area for many CPA firms. I got grandfathered into the CFE program—my experience and qualifications met their standards. There's about 10,000 CFEs now throughout 25 different countries around the world—some with accounting backgrounds, some lawyers, many with criminology or law enforcement backgrounds. Not bad for a professional program that just started in 1988. Certified Fraud Examiner ... it's got a certain ring to it. My thoughts jarred back to our conversation as Tom finished his lunch and went to get some IBC rootbeer.

"Listen, he said, sitting down and giving me a mug filled with amber-colored rootbeer. "What does Dutch have to do with that murdered artist of yours? What's his name? Teddy Noren?"

"I don't know. I can't see Dutch shooting someone—and then painting a picture."

"And Dutch wouldn't cook-up a suicide angle. He'd just shoot the guy and disappear."

I drank the fresh cold rootbeer. It felt cool going down my throat. "We'll figure it out."

"Are you going to tell Lloyd Henderson that Dutch has that 50 grand?"

"I don't think so. I was told to deliver it and that's what I did."

"What now?"

"You stick to the office for now. I'm going to call on Myra Riley."

"When do I get to stick to you?"

"The 24 hours isn't up yet."

"How old is this Myra?"

"Over 40."

"Too old for me. But when I get to be your age ..."

※※※

"She can't stay put," Myra said. "Had a modeling job this morning. She should be home soon."

"Do you know a Dutch Selgado?" I watched her face, especially her eyes.

She shook her head. "No."

"Marilyn never mentioned him?"

"No. I'm sure of it. Why?"

"Well, according to your financial records, a Dutch Selgado loaned your gallery $520,000, and you still owe him $120,000."

"What?" she clutched my hand. "I know nothing about it. Maybe Marilyn borrowed the money."

"He's not exactly a Wall Street banker."

She withdrew her hand. She was getting tense. "That's between our creditors and Marilyn. We sometimes have cash flow difficulties Mr. Cramer." Her voice was scornful, yet laced with dignified embarrassment.

"Could Marilyn be selling fake paintings in your gallery? Laundering money from drugs?"

"Oh, no! Never!"

Just then Marilyn walked in, laden with groceries. She didn't seem too glad to see me. Myra helped her put things away in the kitchen. Then we all sat and had iced tea.

I studied them. Mother and daughter. There was a resemblance, all right. Marilyn was younger and built for speed. But when it came to endurance, my money was on Myra. I had a feeling Marilyn would burn herself out within a few years.

"Have you seen Bram or Frank?" I asked her.

"I saw Bram yesterday. He was very cordial. I think you see ghosts in closets."

"Maybe."

"I do wish you would listen to Dr. Cramer," Myra said. "He's experienced in these matters."

"What matters? Mom, we're all chasing shadows. Teddy killed himself, period. It's difficult enough. Just let me get over it."

"It would simplify everything," I said. "Let's hope you're right." I lifted my glass to my mouth. "Do you know Dutch Selgado?"

Her face was wooden. Her eyes were on me, but I couldn't see anything in them.

Her lips moved slightly? "No."

Myra wanted to change the subject. "It's too early for dinner." She took hold of my hand. "You're eating with us, aren't you?"

"Sure."

Later we had dinner. Myra wasn't a bad cook. After dinner Marilyn announced she had a date. "And I'll leave you two alone."

Myra wanted me to stay longer, but I said no. I promised we'd see a movie and have dinner tomorrow night. Before I left the apartment I called the office. Tom was there.

"I think you forgot about me."

"Who, me?" I feigned.

"I was questioning some suspects. You know Fiddlers' Green on 38th Street?"

"Uh huh."

"Meet me there. We need to talk."

"Okay." I said to Tom.

"Okay." He hung up.

Tom was already there. We sat in a booth. The table held a bowl of pretzels. "You'd better stay at my place tonight," Tom suggested.

"That's no good," I said. "Hiding in a cave isn't going to help. If I can get Dutch to talk—"

"He'll talk with a .38."

"He did say I was suckered. I want to know what he meant by that."

"Why don't you go to his place and ask?"

"His place?"

"While you were playing Romeo, I was doing some work," Tom announced proudly. "Nothing like a telephone to get answers from buddies. Dutch has a joint called the Levantine on 53rd Street. He's also got a new flame named Josephine."

"How did you get all this?"

"The grapevine," Tom said. "I have friends who have their ears wired."

The Levantine had a tuxedoed doorman who looked somewhat like a gorilla in black-tie formal. He nodded at us and opened the door as we walked in. The first thing you smelled was cigarette smoke. Then you smelled limes, rum, and beer. Like a cheap nightclub out of a dime novel.

The blaring music hit you as you walked into the main room. It was loud. A live band was performing on a platform at the far end. The lead singer was a female. One of the electric guitars looked as if it was made out of polished black onyx. It had a flowing, red scarf tied to the end of the neck. No way to make a living. There was a service bar, and tables and booths. Three waitresses scurried about with trays. Dutch was at a central table with two men and a woman. The woman had black hair, a nice soft face, and was wearing a blue dress like a tabloid starlet.

As we walked to a booth Dutch saw me, but his face was impassive. The woman glanced at me and then turned away. She put a hand on Dutch's arm and said something. She looked 40, but was just over it.

A waitress in a cocktail outfit came to our booth. We ordered ginger ale and a virgin pina colada, and she went away.

"How do you like Dutch's girl friend?"

"I like her fine. That black hair looks nice. But it's a wig. Take it off and you'll find a blonde. A honey blonde named Sandra Henderson."

Tom didn't turn his head to look at Sandra. He was too trained for that. "What gives?"

"You've got me."

No sooner had the waitress brought us our drinks, when Dutch was at our booth. He put a meaty hand on the red lacquered table. He ignored Tom, spoke to me. "You got a big mouth, professor." Oblique light made his face more menacing than it was, emphasizing heavy eyebrows, the full lips of his face. "Spreading my name around. I don't think I can trust you." The people at his table were looking our way. Except for Sandra-Josephine. She was looking down at her table, at the drink in her hand, at the band, anywhere but at us.

"What are you talking about?"

"Don't hand me that act."

Tom's forearm was under the table. "If you think you can't trust me," I said, "then I'll just have to refuse your generous offer."

He looked smugly at Tom for the first time. "This guy is a real lulu." He saw Tom's wooden face. Maybe he sensed Tom had a gun on him. He straightened up, his lips twisting into a sinister grin. "I don't like trouble in my place. I'll deal with you later. You bums drink all you want, and be sure you have a good time. You're my guests, see?"

"One question, Dutch," I said. "You said I was suckered into this mess. What did you mean by that?"

"Did I say that? You're mistaken, pal. Just have a good time, and spend your money." He walked confidently back to his table.

Tom's right hand came into sight.

"You had a gun on him?"

"It sorta slipped into my hand," Tom said. The waitress came and took away our glasses.

"This joint is boring," Tom complained.

"Just keep an eye on Dutch's table."

Dutch's girlfriend murmured something to him and got up from the table. She glided past waitresses and customers who were looking for tables and booths. I slid away from the booth and followed her. She went into the ladies' room. I waited.

Two women with men old enough to be their fathers walked past. I waited.

When Sandra came out I confronted her. "I want to talk to you."

"I'm afraid I don't know you."

"Look, Sandra—"

"My name is Josephine."

"All right, Josephine."

She looked worried. "Not now." She came close to me. "Not now."

"When?"

"Tomorrow afternoon. I'll call your office."

"You'd better."

She gave my arm a squeeze with her geranium-red painted fingernails and slipped past me. The pieces of the puzzle were not fitting together any better.

I went back to my booth. Tom and the waitress were acting as if they were involved in deep conversation. She smiled at me. Her hair was auburn, and her face was powdered with freckles.

I sat down. "Sandra or Josephine will call the office tomorrow. I think she's scared."

"That doesn't surprise me." Tom said skeptically.

"Scared I'll blow her plans out of the water. She has to talk to me."

"She'll probably give you a brush off."

"Maybe."

Dutch and his crowd left their table and walked out. "Too bad we couldn't get that money from him," Tom said.

"You want to try?"

"No, thanks. I'm not that crazy."

The night air was getting cool by the time we left the Levantine. The doorman signaled to a cab for us. Tom gave him a dollar.

"We did put in a full day," I remarked.

Tom gave the driver my address.

"Didn't get a thing out of Dutch," I said bitterly. "Except finding out Sandra wears a black wig and looks like she's leading a secret escapade as Dutch's girl. We really didn't get very much."

Nine

Accounting for management is not management, and it should not be thought of as such. But accounting can be made to serve managerial purposes ... and it can help management to do a better job than could be done without it.

—William J. Vatter

The next morning, in my accounting office, I noticed for the first time a spider's web on the ceiling, in a dusty corner. My first impulse was to get a broom and sweep it away. That was what people normally did when seeing a spider's web. But I didn't. I studied the web but didn't see the spider. Where was he hiding? Or she? What did I know about spiders anyway?

If I got rid of that web, the spider would only spin another one. What was I going to be, a home wrecker? No, let the spider alone. He or she probably had a lease anyway—just no rent control. I really missed my daughter. I would be glad when she would be home for summer vacation—assuming she didn't decide to go to summer school.

I could dwell on what I was working on but that would only give me a headache. It was too jumbled. Too many pieces.

And too many questions to be answered. There had to be a fatal flaw somewhere.

Why was Teddy Noren killed? Why leave an oil painting in the artist's apartment? An artist who mostly used acrylics? Who had done the painting? Bram Walker? Frank Masters? Another artist, one I hadn't met? What was the connection to the art gallery? Were fake paintings being sold in order to cover up drug money transactions?

Who was blackmailing Lloyd Henderson? I couldn't see Dutch Selgado in that role, even if he had ended up with the 50 grand. Henderson was a money man, but where did he fit into the financial puzzle?

And I couldn't forget Sandra's dual identity. Sandra and Paul Manfred. Sandra and Dutch; Sandra in a black wig. Did Dutch know full well that his Josephine was actually Sandra Henderson, daughter of the one and only Lloyd Henderson?

What was Sandra's web?

I supposed when I had the answers it would all be clear as primary earnings per share under APB-15—if and when I got the answers.

Then I saw him. From where I sat he was just a red dot, but I saw him all right, crawling along one of the threads.

All those threads to build a web. The web reminded me of a job order cost system functioning properly. You must be able to identify each job physically and segregate all of the costs of the job. Direct materials and direct labor, just like the strands of a web, are carried to the particular job number. Maybe the spider was factory overhead being applied to the job based upon a predetermined factory overhead application rate. No, that's stretching it too much. Like my brain feels right now.

All my deep thoughts of web-erian allegory vanished at the insistently annoying jangle of the telephone. It was Henderson.

"I haven't heard from you."

"It was delivered. That's all I can say now."

"Did you get a look at the man."

"A dwarf. A go-between."

"I'm in the city, in my office, in case you have to talk to me."

"You didn't hear from anyone?"

"No. I would tell you if I had." He hung up.

An hour later Sandra called. "Where do we meet?"

"You tell me."

"Have you told my father ..."

"No," I replied.

"Let's have lunch somewhere. I'm in town. The automat on 42nd Street?"

It was the only automat left in New York. "In an hour?" I said.

"Yes."

"Don't wear your wig," I chided.

Tom was in our accounting office. I told him where I would be with Sandra, and he should follow her when we parted.

Sandra was at a corner table, waiting. We took trays and went down the cafeteria-style line to get what we wanted to eat, and went back to the table. She had a large carnelian ring on her right hand.

We talked as we ate.

"You have to understand what I've gone through for years catering to my father," she said. "I was stagnating. I had to break free. But not at the expense of alienating my father. I went out with Paul a few times for dinner and some dancing. Paul couldn't always get away. Then I went on my own, with a black wig. I met Dutch. He's almost 15 years older than me, but I found him such a thrilling contrast to my sheltered life. He gave me attention. He liked me, and liked showing me off. That is all there is to it."

She saw I didn't believe her, so she shrugged and finished her lunch. "You have me in a bind, what can I say. What do I have to do to keep you quiet?"

"Tell me the truth."

"But I have," she protested.

"What are you and Dutch planning for your father?"

"Nothing."

"Dutch has 50 grand of your father's money. Blackmail money. And you expect me to believe that you don't know anything about it?"

"I don't, Lenny."

"Why the black wig?"

"A whim."

"Does Dutch know who you are?"

"No. How could he?"

"Does Paul Manfred know you're seeing Dutch?"

"No."

"Your father doesn't suspect anything?"

"I'm extremely ... careful."

"Some coincidence. You meet Dutch, go out with him, and he puts the bite on your father. But he doesn't know who you are. And you expect me to buy all that?"

"Fifty thousand dollars is small change to Dutch."

Those were my feelings, too. I'm sure he had bigger criminal operations than what even Tom's network knew. But what was the answer? How much truth was there in what she was telling me? If I pressed her, she might manufacture another lie to cover the first ones. Would she even know the truth if she stumbled on it? To some people, truth is whatever is expedient to say at the moment. Whatever they think will make them look good. "I think I'll get another cup of coffee."

"Go ahead. Would you get me another one also?"

She said I had her in a bind, but she didn't seem very afraid. Was it all a stall? Was Dutch using her, or were she and Paul using Dutch? Dutch wasn't the kind of person to be used or played for a sucker.

I came back with the coffee and sat down.

"What are you going to do?" she said as she spooned sugar into her cup.

"I don't know yet."

"I don't have money to pay you." Topaz eyes glowed with something akin to hate. Then she laughed shrilly. She didn't finish her coffee. She stood up. She put her palms on the table and leaned over, eyes taunting on mine. "Every man has his price. You make up your mind, Lenny." She stalked out of the automat.

People were eating food and gulping down coffee. No one was wearing shorts. They would when it was the middle of May. The summers were getting longer, it seemed. That was fine with me. I was getting hungry again for a ham on cheese sandwich.

Outside, at a phone booth, I slid in a quarter and got the office. "Any messages?" I asked Hildy.

"Marilyn Riley called twice. Wants to see you. That's about it."

I thanked her and took a metro bus downtown. I went to Marilyn's apartment in Soho.

She was in shorts and a t-shirt. "Too early for shorts," I said.

"Sit down. Want a drink?"

I sat down. I didn't want a drink. "You wanted to see me?"

Her hair was loose about her shoulders. "I had a talk with Bram today. I told him I won't sell for him anymore. He said I had no choice. He said if I tried to quit he would go to my grandfather."

"Did he kill Teddy?"

"Nobody killed Teddy."

"What about the oil painting?"

She said she didn't know.

"Why would Teddy want to kill himself?"

"I don't know. I thought a lot about it. I don't have any answers."

"Why is money disappearing from your mother's art gallery?"

"Art is depressed. We're not selling much. Money is hard to come by these days."

"Tell me about the loan from Selgado."

She rose to her feet and started pacing. "I can't cope with this. She put the back of her hand to her forehead for a moment. I'm not a strong person. I thought I could handle it. This just isn't happening to me. Look, you have to do something. I can't let Bram go to my grandfather."

I thought of Paul Manfred. "I don't think Bram will get within two blocks of him."

"If you're thinking of Paul, forget it. Paul does what Sandra tells him to."

"What a tangled family."

"All right. I'm all right," she said hastily, taking short, quick breaths. She sat down again, her face in her hands. Her body was shaking noticeably.

"Are you that afraid of Bram?"

She looked at me and a forced grin was pasted on. "I'm more afraid of my grandfather than Bram. He can be merciless."

"According to your mother, he cares for you."

"As much as he can care for anyone," she retorted. "Will you see Bram, talk to him or something?"

"What you really want me to do is scare him off." I was tired of her, tired of this whole crazy family. What was I accomplishing? Too many loose threads. Too many forks in the road. Too many unexplained variances from standard costs. A variance is the difference between *actual* results and *planned* results in a business organization. Management uses variance analysis to control the costs of production.

The trouble with cost accounting is variance analysis, I thought cynically. When comparing actual direct labor hours in a plant with standard direct labor hours, minimizing idle time does not necessarily maximize profit. It's better to have idle time than to have too much inventory. Most systems do not penalize managers for maintaining too much inventory; they actually reward it. Most systems also penalize managers for idle time. Thus, most managers would rather increase inventory in order to reduce idle time.

Under the full (or, absorption) costing system that most companies use (and as required by the IRS) increasing last-quarter production increases ending inventory levels. This actually reduces reported cost of goods sold, relative to a variable costing system—thus increasing the current year's reported profits—until the effect reverses itself in the next year. Consider the following example, where variable costs of production are $1.50 per unit, and fixed costs of production are $50,000 divided over 100,000 units produced, or $0.50 per unit. Assume a First In First Out (FIFO) physical flow of inventory:

Full Costing:

Sales (100,000 units × $3)		$300,000
Beginning inventory	(10,000 units × $2.00)	$ 20,000
Add: Cost of production	(100,000 units × $2.00)	200,000
Less: Ending inventory	(10,000 units × $2.00)	20,000
Cost of goods sold	(100,000 units)	200,000
Net income		$100,000

Variable Costing:
Sales (100,000 units ×$3)			$300,000
Beginning inventory	(10,000 units × $1.50)	$ 15,000	
Add: Cost of production	(100,000 units × $1.50)	150,000	
Less: Ending inventory	(10,000 units × $1.50)	15,000	
Cost of goods sold	(100,000 units)		150,000
Contribution margin			$150,000
Fixed costs			50,000
Net income			$100,000

If managers increase production, in order to reduce idle time of production workers, under a full costing system (also changing fixed costs per unit to say, $50,000 / 125,000 units = $0.40) observe what happens to cost of goods sold and profit:

Full costing:
Sales (100,000 units ×$3)			$300,000
Beginning inventory	(10,000 units × $2.00)	$ 20,000	
Add: Cost of production	(125,000 units × $1.90)	237,500	
Less: Ending inventory	(35,000 units × $1.90)	66,500	
Cost of goods sold			191,000
Net income			$109,000

Variable Costing:
Sales (100,000 units ×$3)			$300,000
Beginning inventory	(10,000 units × $1.50)	$ 15,000	
Add: Var. cost of prod.	(125,000 units × $1.50)	187,500	
Less: Ending inventory	(35,000 units × $1.50)	52,500	
Variable cost of goods sold			150,000
Contribution margin			$150,000
Fixed costs			50,000
Net income			$100,000

Thus, increasing inventory, without a corresponding increase in sales, will increase current year reported profits under full costing. Neat trick. The IRS requires full costing, of course.

The $9,000 difference in profit between the full and variable costing systems can be reconciled as follows. The 10,000 unit beginning inventory was produced during the previous time period. But under a FIFO physical flow assumption, it was sold during the current time period. Thus, the beginning inventory carries $0.50 per unit, or a total of $5,000 of last period's fixed production costs into the current period's cost of goods sold.

On the other hand, the 35,000 unit ending inventory was produced during the current time period. It is still unsold, and will carry $0.40 per unit, or $14,000 of current period fixed production costs on the balance sheet as an asset until it is sold during the next time period. At that time, it will become a part of cost of goods sold for that year. Therefore, $5,000 of last year's fixed costs are carried into the current year's cost of goods sold, while $14,000 of this year's fixed costs are deferred on the balance sheet and carried into next year's cost of goods sold. The difference is a net reduction in current year cost of goods sold of $9,000—thus increasing current year profit by $9,000. Or, more succinctly:

Beginnng inventory: (10,000 units x $0.50)	$ 5,000
Ending inventory: (35,000 units x $0.40)	(14,000)
Net reduction in costs of goods sold	$ (9,000)

And interpreting variances. Just because a variance looks unfavorable, doesn't mean someone did something wrong. On the other hand, just because we have a favorable variance, doesn't mean something was done right. The standards used could be bad. What's more, think of the production manager faced with having to use up a load of inferior quality raw materials. No matter how efficient a job he does getting quality product out of the materials, his usage variance will look unfavorable next to the budget.

At the same time, the purchasing agent who bought the shoddy materials will be boasting about his *coup* in getting such a great buy on the materials—look at his favorable materials price variance. Not only that, there had been a stock-out, and he was thrilled just to be able to get a timely shipment in under rush order conditions.

And why? The sales manager had brought in an unexpectedly large order, and the production budget hadn't anticipated the demand. Beside, the sales manager was proud of his favorable sales quantity variance. After all, the order had been brought in at the last minute by one of the company's biggest customers. They said if we couldn't meet their order, they'd take it down the street to one of our competitors. Thought he'd done a pretty good job to snag the order. Earned a healthy commission on the sale too. If I had a dog, I'd name it Fifo.

"Will you see him?"

She jarred my thoughts from their theoretic digression. "What good will that do? Just more idle time," I said.

"It might help," she said hurriedly. "Bram's not tough. Even if he is mixed up in sleazy business. You're getting paid to help us, aren't you?"

Even if I did try to warn off Bram Walker in some way, would that change things for Marilyn? She'd get hooked on other creeps as greedy as Bram Walker and Frank Masters. If this little fly managed to escape out of this web, she would only fly right into another one. I had met people like Marilyn before. The woods were full of them. Classic codependent. They thought they were tough cookies, but always crumbled when the going got tough. I stood up. "Okay. I'll talk to Bram. But I can't promise you anything. I can't exactly slug him and heave him onto a train headed west."

"I understand," she said.

"Now, tell me about the loan by Dutch to the art gallery."

She looked surprised. "What is there to tell. We needed the money. I borrowed it from Dutch. There's no law against borrowing money."

"What rate of interest are you paying?" I asked quietly and steadily.

"I don't remember. I'll have to look at the note."

"Did your mother know about the loan?"

"I believe so. She keeps tight control over everything about the gallery. Don't let her fool you. She's no dummy when it comes to accounting."

❖❖❖

I saw Nadja hurrying out of her apartment building. She didn't see me. She was in light blue designer pants and a matching blue shirt with a string of white pearls around her neck. The pearls danced as she suddenly dashed across the street and got into a waiting car. The driver was a young woman. The car sped off.

It was afternoon and the sun was warm. I wished I was back in the library working on a managerial accounting literature review. I went to see Bram Walker.

He wasn't seeing anyone. Not today. Not tomorrow. Not ever. His door was ajar, and I walked into his apartment. He greeted me with a dead silence.

The gun was on the carpet near his body, and there was blood. His eyes were stark open, looking out at eternity. I would bet anything that his fingerprints were on that gun. Looked like another suicide. I went through the place. No scales, no paraffin, and no forgeries this time. Oil paintings on canvases, an easel, brushes, tubes of paint and that was about it. There was a thin, oval palette on the floor. Near it was a palette knife with red paint on the blade. It was time to beat it. So much for warning Bram off for Marilyn.

Outside, in the afternoon sun, I walked slowly. People always remember a man running or walking too fast. Somebody would remember Nadja. I strolled along, thinking. Teddy Noren dead. Bram Walker dead. Two artists. Had some serial killer decided to rid the world of artists? Was Frank Masters still alive? I would pay Mr. Masters a visit. What would be my reason for visiting Frank? I couldn't very well say: just wanted to make sure you were still alive. That wouldn't do. I would think of something by the time I got there.

The law said I should report a dead body. Somebody else would have to have that pleasure. I didn't want a mob of cops on my neck just now. The daily newspaper would say: "Columbia Professor finds Dead Artist."

Frank Masters was in. Surprisingly he was in a jovial mood. "Come in," he said. "Sit down. And where is the fair maid Marilyn?"

I sat down. "I just left her on a merry-go-round, licking an ice cream cone."

"A beautiful image but a child's emotions."

"The kind you can manipulate," I said.

"I suppose some people would be like that." He was on the divan, comfortable, a genial host. "But you didn't come here to talk about Marilyn, did you?"

"To tell you the truth, I'm looking for Nadja," I said.

"I haven't seen the her all day."

"Have you talked with Bram Walker today?"

"Yes," he said. "But he hasn't seen Nadja."

"When was this?"

"About an hour ago. Is it so important?"

"I just wanted to ask her a couple of questions," I said, finishing my drink. "Did Bram tell you Marilyn wanted out?"

"Mr. Cramer, why do you meddle in other peoples' affairs?" He wasn't so genial now. "I don't mind a friendly visit now and then; I like pleasant company. But interfering with peoples' lives—that's a different matter."

"One of my bad habits," I said. "Where can I find Nadja?"

"I don't know. I told you."

"Does she have an address?"

"Try Bram's."

"Does Nadja know a small dark woman with short-cropped black hair?" I said. "About 30 or so?"

He stared at me, unsmiling. "You do get around, don't you, Mr. Cramer?"

"Then you know her?" I countered.

"I know of someone who fits that description," he said easily. "We call her the Princess."

"Princess?"

"She claims she's of royal blood. Russian nobility. What a laugh. I wouldn't be surprised if she was Sheila Shultz of Brooklyn."

"But she does have a name?"

"Lona Plantard. She's at the Walton Arms. Third Avenue in the 20's. One of those new buildings that look utterly ridiculous."

I thanked him and left. He seemed glad to be rid of me. I think we both were.

The Walton Arms did look ridiculous. Evidently an architect's chrome and glass monument to himself. There was a doorman who was busy conversing with a bleached-blonde who had on too much makeup. I walked into the small entry way, looked at the names on the mail boxes, took a polished elevator up to the fifth floor.

The Princess was a slim and trim woman with large liquid saucers for eyes. She wore an off-white satin blouse and tailored black pants. There was a slight accent to her voice but I couldn't quite place it. It certainly wasn't Russian. She looked me up and down scornfully. "What do you want?" she snapped in a tight metallic voice.

"I'd like to talk to Nadja, I said.

"She is not here."

"Okay. She's not here. Do you know where she is?"

"I do not know. I haven't see her in ages."

"You drove her away from Bram Walker's place," I said. "Where did you take her?"

Her eyes were frigid. "I'm afraid you are mistaken."

"It's okay, Princess," I heard Nadja say. "Let him in. We don't want any trouble."

The Princess let me in. She smelled of jasmine. Nadja had been behind the door. She didn't look happy. "So you saw me?" she said.

I sat down in an overstuffed chair. "Correct. Running away like that. Looks mighty suspicious."

The Princess put her hands on her hips and shot daggers with her eyes at me. She looked at me and spoke to Nadja. "Who is this fool? What does he want?"

"An accountant," Nadja said. "And a fraud examiner. He works for Marilyn's grandfather. He must have spotted me leaving Bram's."

"You don't have to talk to him," the Princess said. "Shall I throw him out?"

The Princess took a step towards me. "I wouldn't if I were you." I'd just about had it with the Princess.

"Oh, rats," Nadja said wearily.

"I want to talk to you in private," I told Nadja.

"I will not leave," the Princess said adamantly.

"Princess, please," Nadja pleaded. "You're not making things easier."

The Princess stalked off to a bedroom and slammed the door shut. No doubt she was keeping her ear against the door.

"Why don't you sit down and take it easy?" I said to Nadja.

"I'd rather stand."

"Who is this Princess?"

"A friend of mine."

"Good enough. You were in Bram's apartment, weren't you?"

"You know I was."

"How long were you there?"

"Only a few minutes," she said. "Bram called me earlier, told me he had to see me. He knew I was visiting the Princess. Princess drove me over. I found him dead."

"How long did you stay?"

"Not long. I saw that he was dead. I was scared and ran right out."

"You had no idea what he wanted?"

"No."

She was fingering her pearls. She wasn't ready to jump through hoops. But she was talking to me. That was certainly an improvement.

"You think he killed himself?"

She said it looked that way, but she didn't think so.

I asked her why she thought that, and she said there was no reason for him to kill himself. And where did the gun come from? He didn't own a gun.

"Did he have a falling out with Frank Masters?" I asked her. She was surprised at the question.

"They were the best of friends."

"But you know they were into dealing crack—and some of it was just wax?"

Nadja shrugged. "They needed money to live. But it's hard to get recognition as an artist, because there are so many—especially here in New York. There are lots of people in the art world who are willing to sell crack on the street because they're desperate for money."

"Who is their source?"

"I don't know."

94

"Dutch Selgado?"

"I told you I don't know."

"Bram, Frank and Teddy were artists and friends. Teddy gets killed, and now Bram. You don't think that's rather funny?"

"Death is not funny," she snapped.

"You know what I mean."

"What do you want me to say?"

I leaned back and looked up at her. "Nadja, you're not stupid. You're up to your ears in this mess. The police will learn that you were his girlfriend and sooner or later they'll find you. What are you going to tell them?"

"I didn't have anything to do with Bram's death."

"You ran away. Somebody must have seen you. The police will know. You're a suspect, Nadja."

Just then the bedroom door flew open, and the Princess came charging across the room at me, her face contorted with rage and hate. I bounced out of the chair to meet her head on. She scratched at my face and tried to kick me. I twisted my body quickly so her foot sailed into my knee. My leg buckled and I dropped to the floor in pain. So much for sedentary life styles.

Nadja kept screaming for us to stop, and succeeded in pulling Princess away.

I got to my feet and went into the bathroom to wash the blood off of my face. I could hear Nadja and the Princess screaming at each other.

I went back into the room. "Knock it off. Both of you. You want the neighbors to call the police?"

They stared at me, Nadja looking dumb, the Princess glaring with hate dripping from her eyes.

I said to Nadja, "Why is she so protective of you?" I jerked a thumb at the Princess. "Is she your mother?"

The Princess stared at me.

"Oh please," Nadja wailed.

I looked at Nadja. "Maybe you wanted out too and Bram said no so you killed him." I didn't really believe that but it was something to say.

"Get out," the Princess shouted.

I left. My face was hurting. Shaving was definitely not going to be fun tomorrow morning.

Ten

Unless the firm recognizes differences in cost behavior among segments, there is a significant danger that incorrect or average-cost pricing will provide openings for competitors. Thus cost analysis at the segment level must often supplement analysis at the business unit level.

—Michael E. Porter

Tom was waiting for me at our accounting office. His gray suit coat was hung over the back of a chair, and he had rolled up his white shirt sleeves. "Hot today," he said. "Where have you been?"

I told him.

"It gets crazier and crazier." He scratched his head. "I followed that blonde, Sandra, after she left the automat. Went to the Levantine, left there, alone, to Grand Central. Took a train to Long Beach. I made sure she left with the train and came back here."

"Two suicides or two murders," I said. "Both corpses in the cocaine racket."

"Looks like someone is muscling into the territory," Tom said.

"Drug related hits?" I said. "Could be. I just don't think so. Their customers seemed to be small-time."

"Yeah, hit men don't usually leave their weapons behind. But if they were drug related killings—my bet is on Dutch Selgado."

"He fits in somewhere. But where?"

"Listen, Dutch said you were suckered in," Tom said. "Don't you see? You find two bodies. Two, mind you. Do you report either one? No. Serious ethics violations, Lenny.

And totally illegal. And what is your excuse? You were protecting your clients. Myra Riley. Lloyd Henderson. Privilege exists for accountants only in the State of Texas, Lenny. You know in New York all you've got is a confidential relationship with your clients. Here, only lawyers have advocacy privilege—and even that doesn't excuse violating the law."

I was already ahead of Tom, but I let him continue. "If the police discount the suicide angle, then who's the fall guy? Who found the bodies? Who delivered the money? Some coincidence. Why should the cops buy some crazy story? You were just protecting clients. Right. By not reporting the bodies, you broke the law. Being a Ph.D. won't help you. If you would go that far for your clients, why not further? Let's say the two rip-off, crack-dealing artists were major threats to your clients somehow. So you knocked them off. That's reasonable for a jury to take it that way. Dutch had to be in on it, because he knew you were being set up. Either that or he found out and wanted some of the action for himself. If that isn't being suckered in, I don't know what is."

Tom was no junior, greenshade forensic accountant. He had street savvy and a clear head. He knew how to cut through the incessant smoke and mirrors.

"A good theory," I said. "It fits perfectly. Sure. But we still don't know why they were killed. Who'd they rip-off with the wax, and where's the payback? We don't even know who killed them. If your theory is correct, then Lloyd Henderson is behind it all. But what does he want? It can't be financial gain. He has more money than he can count."

"The more you have, the more you want."

Abruptly I reached for the phone and got in touch with Henderson. He was still in his office. I told him I would be right over.

"Want me to go with you?" Tom asked.

"No. Marilyn and her friends were probably aggregating a lot of small drug sales, and covering the cash proceeds for Dutch by staging the sale of a fake work of art through her mother's gallery, and then making a 'loan repayment'. Go back to the art gallery and check the invoices for all of the paintings purchased over the past two years. See if any came from the corpses, from Henderson, or from *any* suspicious source. There has to be a connection to the art forgery angle. Match the purchase invoices with the sales invoices and verify the related cash flows. Confirm the actual existence of any repeat-buyers, and watch for sales timed closely with repayments on Selgado's loan. I'll call after I see King Midas."

"Just don't fly off the handle," Tom cautioned. "He'll bury you if he thought you're going to stand in his way, and nobody will ever know what happened to you."

❖❖❖

Paul Manfred took me to Henderson's office. He was as silent as the tomb.

Lloyd Henderson was standing by a shelf full of brightly jacketed books. He had on a pale blue neatly tailored suit. "What is the urgency, Dr. Cramer?"

"Another suicide," I said, not bothering to sit down. "Teddy Noren and now Bram Walker. Quite unusual, isn't it? Both men were close to your grand daughter."

He moved to a chair and sat down, with an expression that looked like a wise old Indian chief. "You think I know something of these deaths?"

"Very likely," I said.

"Sit down, Dr. Cramer."

I sat down.

"I did not engineer anyone's death, Doctor. You have my word on that. If you think I did, then go to the police."

"I recently found a dead body, a man named Bram Walker. I did not report it. The body may have been found by now. If I went to the police now they would apply a lemon squeezer to my big toe to get a confession. Both men look like suicides. I don't think so. I'm running around chasing financial shadows in the dark, and I don't like it. Perhaps you can enlighten me a little bit."

"You think I hold strings and manipulate puppets?"

"That wouldn't surprise me."

"If I wanted to kill people why would I go to you, Dr. Cramer? I know enough people I could count on to deal with any difficult situation."

"Paul Manfred, for instance?"

His eyes twinkled. "Paul is my personal bodyguard."

"What about Dutch Selgado?"

"He is my daughter Sandra's problem."

"So you know about them?"

"There is not much that I don't know about my family, Dr. Cramer."

"Then what did you bring me in for?" I said bitterly. Was Tom right with his theory? Was I just a sucker being framed by Henderson?

"I need you to find out what few things I don't already know about my family members' clandestine involvements," he said. "My granddaughter Marilyn is being used by someone in order to extort money from me. Money or something else. Wealthy people are vulnerable. You said that yourself, Dr. Cramer."

Henderson paused. "The 50 thousand dollars was obviously a test. So far no one has contacted me for more money. Or anything else. I have three daughters. I despise them all. I let Myra go because she married beneath her. Old fashioned, yes. The point is, she disobeyed me. Sandra and Cora stay with me, not because they have any love for me, but to be sure I don't disinherit them. Greed sits on our shoulders, Doctor, all of the time."

"Or something else," I said. "If money isn't the object, what is? I have a feeling you know."

"I do believe it has to do with a new microchip my people are working on, Dr. Cramer. A new type of memory that will revolutionize the industry."

"Maybe."

He laughed hollowly. "You don't believe me, do you Doctor? Well, no matter. You're on my payroll. I don't have to worry about whether or not you trust me. You see, your partner John Grant, is also greedy. I'm paying him well for your forensic services."

I wondered if he knew about Sandra and Paul Manfred. If he didn't, then that would be a jolt. And where would it get me if I indulged in some gossip?

We didn't shake hands when we parted. Paul Manfred saw me out. Two police officers and a detective were waiting for me at my accounting office.

Bram Walker's body had been found. Two people who knew Nadja swore they had seen her run from the building. They tracked her down to the Princess, and she admitted being in the building. The Princess stuck her two cents in and told the cops I had also been in the apartment, and had come from there to question Nadja. So now the police were here and were not too polite. They were ready to drag me off to the nearest station house for some heavy questioning when John Grant made some rushed phone calls. Grant did have valuable connections. The police were even more steamed, because they didn't like interference from higher-ups. But they lost their enthusiasm for taking me to the station house.

While the police were on my neck with questions, ballistics checked the murder weapon. No fingerprints, but the gun was registered to Paul Manfred. Two detectives went to Henderson's office but did not find Manfred. He had disappeared. His description was in the late editions of both local newspapers, and the next TV cable news broadcasts gave his description.

The police left, but not before I persuaded them to take one of our practice associates along. I persuaded them with John Grant's help. I told him to stay put in Police Plaza and keep his ears opened, while I stayed furtively in my office.

Hildy wanted to stay, but I told her to go on home for the day. Tom brought up dinner for two from a fast-food burger place, and we ate in my office.

I told our assistant in police headquarters to check in every half hour.

He did.

Through the night reports came in from people who had spotted Paul Manfred. It was more like magazine rack Elvis sightings.

He had been seen in the Silk Stocking District, Chelsea, the Village, Brooklyn Heights, Flatbush, Rego Park, Woodhaven, Ozone Park, Orange, New Jersey, Great Neck, and Penn Station.

"It seems he's been seen everywhere but Singapore," I told Tom.

"How did he know the cops were on his tail?"

"Maybe he got a message from the invisible man."

"You think he did it?"

"I don't know what to think. Why kill someone with your own gun and leave it behind?" I said. "That doesn't make sense."

"Nothing in this lopsided engagement makes sense," Tom said. "Are you going to stay here all night?"

"I don't know. But I'd sure like to ask Paul Manfred a few questions right now. Let's hope the police will let me talk to him when they get him."

"With all the connections Grant seems to pull out of the woodwork, they'll probably deliver him to you personally, and have you sign a receipt."

"True. He really came through, didn't he?"

"I'm as shocked as you are." Tom yawned. "But what else could he do? He had to protect his own people. He can't afford not to."

It was the middle of the night and the streets were silent. The moon was far off. Cold, impersonal, floating like a round white haze. Tom took the next call and grimaced. He put down the receiver. "Someone called the police to inform them that he remembers seeing someone who looks like Manfred buying a fishing pole in Howard Beach."

"What else? This is New York."

"You get every imaginable crank calling in when something like this turns up. I'm beat. I've got to sack-out for a while. Where is that cot?"

❂❂❂

In the dawn's early light the city looked somber. The usual haze of amber smog filled the air. But slowly the city started coming to life, little by little the traffic began picking up. That's when I really began to feel it. The heavy paws of exhaustion. Mental, emotional. When Hildy walked in I told her I was going home.

Tom was up and about. "Let's have breakfast."

"I hate morning people. I need sleep."

"You look like you need it—some breakfast might perk you up."

I ignored him and went home.

It was noon when Myra woke me. Her voice had an edge of acid. "What's going on? I've had police coming out of my ears."

"They're looking for Paul."

"I know. But why me?"

"Why not? Paul worked for your father. The police are questioning all of the family members."

"They've been hot and heavy on Sandra," Myra said. "Why her so much? And how did they know she and Paul went out together?"

"I don't know."

"You didn't tell them—"

"Not that. It's a crazy case and they're as stumped as I am."

"Can you come here for lunch?"

"Lunch? I haven't had breakfast yet."

"I need to see you."

"I'll come by in about an hour." I hung up, shaved very gingerly, and took a cold shower. I felt livelier than a corpse, but not much. I put on fresh clothes and went out into a drizzle. This whole engagement was beginning to remind me of the time I inventoried equipment in a hospital morgue. It was my first job as an accounting staff junior.

All of the computerized depreciation records for the hospital had to be verified by checking tag-numbers on the entire hospital's inventory of major-moveable capital equipment—including the morgue. They had to allocate depreciation expense to appropriate departments somehow. It was important for cost reimbursement, based on step-down allocation sheets.

Step-down allocations are used to assign the costs of service departments—like data processing, fiscal administration, and medical records—to revenue producing departments like radiology, clinical pathology, and operating room. The step-down method gets it's name from the way the numbers are arranged on an accounting worksheet. They sort of, step down, like a staircase, for lack of a better description. It's one of the few aesthetic things we do in accounting. Perhaps the illustration on the following page will help.

Allocating service department costs to revenue producing departments allows a full cost measure for the services being sold. Therefore, the relative ability of each salable service to cover all of it's indirect costs and produce a profit can be analyzed. Believe it or not, step-down allocation worksheets have been used by Medicare for years to allocate hundreds of billions of dollars in healthcare payments to hospitals throughout the country. Why did they choose the step-down method? Why not some other method? Just think how accountants can change the massive flow of public resources, just by selecting a different cost allocation method. But, then again, step-down worksheets do have a certain eye-appeal.

Yeah, that same queasy, blah feeling—like lifting a corner of the draped sheet over a stiff on a gurney, so I could check the gurney's tag number by the deceased persons foot. Just blah. It was in the walk-in freezer. Then check the autopsy tables, *etc.* Hmm. Maybe that first assignment's what got me interested in forensic accounting to begin with. That's a morbid thought. Blame it all on step-down allocation worksheets ...

❖❖❖

I arrived at Myra's apartment. She had coffee perking. I had that with some scrambled eggs, and she told me Sandra had been to see her.

"Did she tell you where Paul is now?"

Myra frowned. "No. How would she know? He's probably hiding out somewhere—or maybe he's left the country." She was eating a tuna fish sandwich and fruit salad.

Step-Down Allocation Worksheet

	Service Departments			Revenue Producing Departments			
	Data Processing	Fiscal Admin.	Medical Records	Radiology	Clinical Pathology	Operating Room	Total
Direct costs:	$ 30,000	$ 20,000	$ 10,000	$ 100,000	$ 50,000	$ 80,000	$ 290,000
D.P. Allocation:	(30,000)	1,000	1,500	10,000	8,000	9,500	
	$ 0	$ 21,000					
F.A. Allocation:		(21,000)	1,200	7,000	6,000	6,800	
		$ 0	$ 12,700				
M.R. Allocation:			(12,700)	4,400	4,000	4,300	
			$ 0				
Total:				$ 121,400	$ 68,000	$ 100,600	$ 290,000

"Do you think he could be hiding in that great big house on the Island?"

"The police have been there with a warrant. No Paul. And my father wouldn't hide a criminal, even if it was Paul."

"We don't really know if he is a criminal," I said. "Not counting his past record."

"What does that mean?"

I had a second cup of coffee. "It means, Myra, that even though it was his gun, it doesn't mean he did the shooting."

"I don't follow."

"Somebody could have borrowed Paul's gun, shot Bram Walker, and left the gun behind to implicate your father's bodyguard."

"But why?"

"I told you. To implicate him." My patience was getting thin at this point.

"I mean, why Paul? Where does Paul come into the equation?"

"He has a record. He's made to order as a patsy. The fall guy."

"But—" She bit her lip.

"Yeah," I said. "His gun? Where did he keep his gun? In your father's house, I guess. Who would be likely to get hold of it? A member of your family."

"You mean Sandra?"

"Sandra ... or your father."

"Sandra was close to Paul. We know that. But why should my father frame Paul? He values Paul's loyalty."

"Would he be so fond of Paul if he found out Paul was having an affair with Sandra?"

Myra was confused. Even though her father had kicked her out, she probably still felt a sense of family protectionism. But I could be wrong, of course. There are people who do hate their relatives. Fathers, mothers, brothers, sisters. And sons and daughters. In-laws and outlaws. Lloyd Henderson had told me he despised his daughters. Maybe the feeling was mutual. A family of hate. Sounds like a real fun environment.

"Since you've mentioned Sandra," Myra said, "what about Cora? Why leave her out?"

"So far she's the invisible woman. Either she's out of all of this, or she's extremely clever."

"It's funny but Cora has always been very remote. I could never get close to her. I've tried. I reached Sandra for a while, and then she put up a wall, and that was that. I always hated living in that house. You could feel the ice growing down the walls. My parents had a bitter marriage. My mother died fairly young. I sometimes think about my mother, what she must have gone through—though she had her calculating moments."

Myra wanted me to stay, but I couldn't. I took my leave and went back to the office.

Tom had talked to Shirley, the waitress from the Levantine, Dutch Selgado's joint. He went to have breakfast with her. "I told her my life's story. Then she told me her life's story. That exhausted both of us."

"I can imagine."

"Listen, this kid keeps her ears open." Tom said. "That Sandra babe, who's Josephine when she's got her wig on, well, according to Shirley, she and Dutch are not lovers. In fact, she thinks Dutch hates her guts."

"That's why Dutch likes to show her off?—that was what Sandra told me."

"Aw." Tom shook his head. "Shirley thinks it's all an act. She thinks Sandra has some kind of leverage on Dutch, and Dutch has to play along. That's what Shirley thinks."

"That might answer a few questions," I said. "If Shirley's right."

Tom grinned at me. "You're thinking again."

"We know Dutch wouldn't go for small time stuff, like a $50 thousand blackmail stunt. But what if Sandra had something big on Dutch? What if Sandra is forcing him to go along with some scheme she and Paul Manfred cooked up? That would answer a lot of questions."

Tom shook his head. "If Sandra had something on Dutch, he'd knock her off."

"Blackmailers are too clever for that," I told Tom. "They cover their bases—keep things in safe deposit vaults or hand them over to their lawyers with instructions to open up envelopes in case they meet with suspicious accidents."

"You think Sandra decided to get rid of Paul because she wanted everything for herself?"

"That's not logical," I said. "Paul could always put a monkey wrench in the works if he thought Sandra was turning on him—unless Paul Manfred wasn't in on anything, and Sandra thinks she's playing every side off against the middle."

"But what's she after? Tom asked. "Fifty thousand clams is nothing compared to her half of the estate."

Hildy walked into the room and we used her for a sounding board. We didn't get anywhere.

Our assistant at Police Plaza called. No crank calls for hours. No calls at all pertaining to Paul Manfred. I told him to go home and get some sleep.

"The novelty is wearing off," I told Tom.

"I'd like to know who tipped him off that the cops were coming."

"There's always the back door," I said to Tom. Tom got up.

"Do I have to work tonight?" he asked.

"I suppose I can spare you."

"Some people work regular hours."

"Got a date with Shirley?" I razzed.

"Yeah. She's off tonight. Of course, I'm mixing business with pleasure. Between heart throbs I'll ask about our pal Dutch. Shirley isn't too keen on him. Tried to make a pass once, and Shirley fended him off."

"Sure. She was waiting for a millionaire like you."

Tom pretended to be hurt and left.

I went home, packed, and took an afternoon flight to Dallas-Fort Worth. A taxi took me to Green Oaks Inn, just off Interstate 30. I met Rick Mannino at 9:00 in the Feather's restaurant. It had a dance floor and a sunken bar in the middle. Rick Mannino was my contact person at General Dynamics Corporation, a defense contractor with more than 22,000 employees in the Fort Worth area.

Mannino outlined my expert witnessing chore in a straightforward fashion. "Look we have a number of projects in our Fort Worth plant. Some projects are based upon a fixed-price contract and others are based upon a cost-reimbursement approach. We have a security service that costs about $2 million each year. How should this amount be allocated to our various contracts?"

Mannino paused and smiled briefly. He was about six feet, four inches and weighed about 200 pounds. He had a full head of dirty blond hair. "Of course, the government would like for the total $2 million to be allocated to the fixed-price contracts—such as our Soviet MIG airplane simulator project. G.D.C. would prefer to allocate it to the cost-plus contracts—such as our night pulse-laser sighting system."

"So my job is to testify on the proper allocation of security costs among all of your various contracts in progress? With the break-up of the Soviet Union, why have a MIG simulator?"

"Right for the first question. As to the second, most of those republics are still unstable. Plus the Commonwealth—especially Russia—needs the money. They're selling MIGs to many countries, such as India and much of the Middle East. Now suppose I let you get some sleep tonight, and I'll pick you up in the morning at 8:00. We'll tour some of our plants and let you ask questions. I'm sure the government lawyer will ask you if you've even been in our plant."

After Mannino said good-bye, I went to the fifth floor and passed out cold for the night on the surprisingly comfortable hotel bed.

On Friday Mannino took me on a tour of the Fort Worth G.D.C. facilities off Highway 341. With over 22,000 employees, there were at least 20 buildings with a mile long assembly plant. Security guards were stationed everywhere, many with fully automatic rifles. Throughout the day I referred to my blue copy of **Government Contract Guidebook**, by D.P. Arnauas and W.J. Ruberry.

There were several ways to allocate the security costs:

1. Based upon floor space in the buildings
2. Based upon the amount of labor cost of the project
3. Based upon direct engineering hours
4. Based upon direct manufacturing labor hours
5. Based upon number of employees
6. Based upon accumulated total cost of the project

From Federal Acquisition Regulations (FAR) Subpart 31.2, I studied the following definition of allocability while I ate my $1.50 burger in one of the big cafeterias at General Dynamics:

> A cost is allocable if it is assignable or chargeable to one or more cost objectives on the basis of relative benefits received or other equitable relationship. Subject to the foregoing, a cost is allocable to a Government contract if it:
>
> (a) Is incurred specifically for the contract;
>
> (b) Benefits both the contract and other work, and can be distributed to them in reasonable proportion to the benefits received; or
>
> (c) Is necessary to the overall operation of the business, although a direct relationship to any particular cost objective cannot be shown.

I spent some time reviewing my Standard Form 1411, which includes cost or pricing data submitted to the federal government. I tentatively decided that the cost of security should be allocated to the various projects based upon relative direct engineering hours.

Mannino indicated that the federal government preferred allocations based upon relative direct manufacturing labor costs.

Around 5:30 Mannino and I passed through the security checkpoints and walked to his car. "They check everyone and everything. They even check your thermos jug, because one employee carried out enough jet plane paint to cover his entire boat," Mannino said.

Mannino had two tickets to see a Rangers' game. On the way to Arlington stadium, we passed the University of Texas at Arlington on Cooper and Mitchell streets, and along the way I noticed a business called "4 Day Tire Store." Why would a tire store wish to close three days out of each week?

Mannino stopped at an automatic teller machine at a Texas Commerce Bank on Border Street for some cash. A Honda in front had a bumper sticker which said "Backing the Blue," referring to the police, and another one, "Support Beef. Run Over a Chicken."

On the way to the Atchafalaya River Cafe we were stopped at a railroad crossing by a fast moving train. "I knew a train engineer once who fell asleep and ran a mile-long coal train through a signal—was a miracle no one got killed. The engineers tie down the dead-man switch so they can sleep on long hauls. System override. Scary. It's a foot pedal that's supposed to trigger the brakes in the event the engineer has a heart-attack or something. So much for the benefits of safety control," I reported matter-of-factly.

Mannino related to me some similar war stories.

From the steps of the restaurant I could see Arlington Stadium with a giant poster of Nolan Ryan on the stadium itself. Mannino proudly said that Nolan had pitched seven no-hitters and had a 10 year contract.

"What a pitching arm," I graciously said, mustering my social skills.

"You know that George Bush, Jr. is part owner of the Texas Rangers," Mannino said.

At that point our waiter arrived and gave us some Mardi Gras beads. I ordered Cajun crawfish bisque, red beans, rice, and sausage. Mannino told me that a Cajun was a Louisiana native descended from French-speaking immigrants from Acadia. My meal was good—hot and spicy.

After moving Mannino's car from the restaurant parking lot to the stadium lot, we walked into Arlington stadium. It was hot—6:30 PM and still 96°. We had excellent seats on the first base side. I could see Six Flags Over Texas from the stadium. There were large Texas (red, white, and blue), American, and City of Arlington flags flying.

It was an outdoor stadium with real, green grass. The souvenir program said it had 42,431 seats. The stadium gradually filled up because number 34 was the starting pitcher—Nolan Ryan. The franchise.

The first wave started in the second inning, but by the third inning the Ryan Express did not go on. He left because of a sore arm. "The guy is still pitching in his forties," Mannino commented. When the Toronto Blue Jays were five runs ahead, I begin looking around at the signs in the stadium—Dr. Pepper, Delta the Orient, Well Made Weller Made, and Enjoy Coca-Cola Classic, among others. I noticed the jet planes flying over from the airport. Someone had a homemade sign: "Juan You're The One." Referring, of course, to Juan Gonzalez.

Soon my biggest thrill was hearing the hot-dog man shout "hot dog." Mannino said he was one of a kind. "He sounds like the Hunch Back of Notre Dame."

During the sixth inning there was a dot race. Three colored dots raced on the score board. Sponsored by Whataburger, my yellow dot card had a chance to win.

For some reason the racing dots looked like they were moving backwards, and reminded me of backflush costing. With the just-in-time system at some companies, the elapsed time between receipt of raw materials and the production of the finished goods is reduced drastically. Work-in-process becomes a small, trivial amount. Thus, an end-of-period cost estimate of the fast-moving work-in process inventory is sufficient for financial reporting.

Backflushing accumulates costs by working backward through the accounting information after production is completed. You work backwards from the end of the accounting period by using end-of-period estimates of the material and conversion components of all unfinished goods. The red dot won the race. Too bad.

"Where do they find blue gloves?" Mannino asked. "Do they cost more than normal gloves?" Several of the Blue Jays' players had blue gloves.

"Well, as I tell my students, when cattle go to the slaughter house, they use everything except the moo."

"The what?"

"Moo. Moo. They cannot sell the moo. The cow goes in one end and steak, hamburger meat, prime rib, tallow for surgical thread, cow hide for baseball gloves and baseballs all come out the other end. Even the blood is used. It's a joint-cost problem."

"So they sell the blood to vampires." Mannino smiled. "How do they price all of the products?" Mannino asked.

"That's a good question. There are various costs that result in a number of products. Just like the oil business. Do you really want to know?"

"Sure." He was apparently bored also.

"Joint costs can be allocated using physical measurements. For example, in the petroleum industry you can use BTU's."

"But a pound of prime rib costs more than hamburger meat," Mannino protested.

"Right. So there are three alternative methods favored by many companies—the net-realizable value method, the constant gross-margin percentage method, and the sales value at split-off method."

"Oh no, I feel a lecture coming." At that moment the crowd began shouting because Juan Gonzalez hit a home run. "Juan was the most valuable player and Rookie of the Year in 1990."

"For the alternative methods, we go to the marketplace and work backward. The net-realizable value is calculated—selling price, less the costs of completion and sale occurring after the split-off point."

"Split-off point?"

"The point where the joint products can be separately identified and where the decision to sell or process any of them further can be made independently of the other products. The joint costs are then allocated based upon this net-realizable value."

"Hot dogs. Hot dogs." The Hunchback of Notre Dame walked by.

"In a similar fashion, if raw products can be sold at the split-off point to other processors, the joint costs may be allocated to the various products based upon relative sales value at the split-off point. Then again, we could simply compute the gross margin percentage for all of the joint products taken together. Then we would impute that percentage margin back on each of the individual products. Next we would simply plug the allocation of joint cost required to give the desired result."

"OK. Which is best?" Mannino asked.

"Each method is arbitrary and is based upon implicit assumptions. But many managers favor the net-realizable-value method. It is based upon the economic characteristics of the joint products. Actually, it's my favorite."

"Let me summarize," Mannino grinned. "I have a mint, 1968 Nolan Ryan rookie baseball card. The last time I checked it was worth $1,500. Trouble is that on one-half of the card is Jerry Koosman."

"Now Koosman pitched for 19 years, winning 222 games, but he's no Hall of Fame material. My question, how do I allocate my $800 cost of the card between Koosman and Ryan?"

"One baseball card worth $1,500," I repeated as I was thinking. "Suggestion. Get a good pair of scissors and cut the card into two parts." I smiled broadly.

Mannino groaned even though he knew I was joking. "Nolan says that Jerry Koosman keeps reminding him that Koosman's Mets rookie card keeps climbing in value. By the way, a mint Mickey Mantle rookie card has sold for as much as $40,000 at auction."

Eleven

Responsibility accounting means that each sale or cost that a company expects during a year is delegated to a department manager and should appear in a departmental budget. The total revenues and costs in all the departmental revenue and expense budgets should equal the total budgeted revenues and costs for the company for the coming year.

—Thomas E. Lynch

The afternoon when I returned to the "Big Apple," John Maple, a homicide detective, called on me. The drizzle outside had long stopped and now it was getting cold. Certainly a contrast to the hot weather in Texas. The detective sat across from me; he was young, built like a bull, with a square face. His hair was a deep black, combed straight back, with artistic waves in it. He didn't look too happy.

"We've been putting two and two together," he said. "A nasty habit we have. There has to be a connection between Walker and Teddy Noren. They knew each other, and they were found dead the same way. So we're ruling out the suicide angle in Noren's death. Two murders. Same *M.O.* Probably by the same person. We're looking for Paul Manfred because the gun found by Walker's body was registered in his name, but that does not mean positively he killed both men or even one."

A very smart cop, I thought.

We traded glances and suddenly he grinned. It made him look boyish. But he still wasn't my best friend. He was about 30 and his skin was tanned. "You're deep in this, Dr.

Cramer. You may not have killed anyone, but you haven't told us everything."

"I told you all I know."

"Do you know where Paul Manfred is now?"

"No. I wish I did."

"Do you think Manfred killed these people?

"No. I think he was framed."

"Why do you think that?"

"I just think it."

"That's not good enough."

Heavy silence then, thick as pea soup.

"Why did you go to see Myra Riley last Thursday?" he said.

So I had been followed. "I don't like eating alone.

His face became grim. "Wrong answer."

"I did ask a couple of questions. But the answers meant nothing."

"Your responses are not what I would call cooperation," he said mildly.

"If something comes up, I'll call you."

"That's mighty nice of you," he retorted.

The sarcasm didn't affect me at all.

"We have a murder case on our hands and no cooperation from anyone. Two murders. This Lloyd Henderson is one of those powerful figures we can't touch because he has a small army of lawyers to shield him. Your boss, Grant, has connections with the D.A.'s office, so we have to handle you with kid gloves. It makes you want to give up."

"He's my partner. I'm a professor. I'm only doing a favor for the President of my university."

He stood up, a frustrated cop, strong, maybe untarnished, with a contempt for people who get away with things, especially culpable people with political pull. He didn't say good-bye. He turned and walked out.

Tom called me half an hour later. "Shirley has a friend," he said.

"Not interested."

"We could have dinner together, maybe take in a movie."

"I don't feel like eating. I don't feel like a movie. I want to get a decent night's sleep tonight." I told him about the visit from the homicide division man. I told him about the tail on me.

"You think the phone is tapped?"

"I don't think so," I said. "Hildy wouldn't let anyone into this office without asking me first."

"You're in the dark ages Lenny. The boys have equipment now you wouldn't believe."

"Okay. So what?"

"Look, I think you should join us. But first, make sure that your tail gets distracted."

"Where do we meet?"

"Columbus Circle. I'll pick you up. In an hour."

"Yes, but—"

Tom had hung up.

If I was being shadowed, then it was by an expert. I used a bus, a subway, and a cab. Tom picked me up in Columbus Circle. There was no one in the car with him.

"I don't think I was followed. If I were, I must have lost him."

"Two men in cars and one man on foot. They're still with you."

"Rats. What do you want? I'm an accountant, not a detective."

"Well the cops think you're important. Doesn't that make you feel great, Lenny? You've got a police escort."

"Can we lose them?"

"You don't think I'd embarrass Shirley and her friend by showing up with a flock of detectives on your tail, do you?"

"Who is this friend?"

"You don't know her," Tom said. "But she's the talkative type." He cut into Central Park. "We don't have to worry about the guy on foot. One of the cars picked him up."

"Now I can breathe easier," I said.

"Give me a break," Tom said. He came out on Fifth Avenue. "Now I'll show you what an expert can do."

It wasn't going to be easy because the cars had to have radio contact. They weren't going to call in the marines because we weren't wanted for anything. It was strictly a surveillance job. No roadblocks, nothing of that nature. Still—two cars. One car wouldn't be so hard, but two—Tom was good at tailing people and at losing tails when he wanted to.

He headed east for Lexington, then downtown to 14th Street, then down the row of blocks where the book stores are huddled like a herd of buffalo. Down Broadway, past City Hall, into the Wall Street district.

By now the police had to know we were trying to lose them. Throwing caution to the wind one of the cars inched forward, tried to climb into our hip pockets.

Then Tom did something cunning. He turned right fast and our back hugging car kept on going. He would circle the block and join the parade, but Tom made another right and then a left and by this time with the semi-gridlock we were in, the driver of the car would never catch us. That left us with just one tail.

"Do I get a raise?" Tom said.

"I'm only second in command," I reminded him. "Just hired help. You'll have to talk to Grant."

"I'm killing myself for nothing." Tom was kidding.

I knew he was enjoying the challenge, however dubious this excursion might be. "Watch out for red lights," I told him. "That's all we need."

"Those red lights better watch out for me." Tom doublebacked and soon we were on Park Row. "We're gonna be late for our date, but I can't help it." Tom swung onto the Brooklyn Bridge.

He made a turn onto another lane and hung on. When we got off the bridge he pulled a U-turn and went back onto it, and soon we were back in Manhattan. He drove through Chinatown, then Little Italy. "Did we lose 'em?"

I looked back. "I think so."

Her name was Shirley Magruder, and her friend was an administrative assistant named Stella Benson. They were waiting for us and were getting a little hungry. Stella was about 25 with black hair that hung like a thick satin curtain down her shoulders. She had nice features and a soft, smooth face, high cheek bones, almost almond shaped eyes.

We went to Peng Teng for dinner. We had the family dinner for four. "I love Chinese food," Stella said.

After finishing everything off with green tea and almond cookies Tom said to Stella, "Tell my professor here about the Princess and Nadja."

So that was why Tom wanted me to join them.

"Oh, no," Stella pouted. "I'm not a blabbermouth."

"He's interested," Tom said.

"There's nothing to tell," Stella said, pouring tea for herself. "I met the Princess through Nadja. At a party. She asked me if I wanted to smoke a rock, and I got very indignant. I told Shirley here about it. When you asked Shirley if she knew anything about Nadja or the Princess, she remembered what I had told her."

"Come on, Stella," Shirley urged. "There's more to it than that."

Stella flared up. "What are you trying to get me to say?"

People were staring. "Let's drop it," I said. "It can't be that important."

After some more small talk Stella began easing her defenses a little. Well, she had sold some rocks, as she called them. It seemed the Princess did the recruiting, and Bram Walker and Frank Masters were middlemen who supplied the crack cocaine. Yes. Stella had met Marilyn and Teddy Noren. Marilyn was one of the street dealers and Teddy did the weighing—and sometimes cutting, with chunks of paraffin. It was one of Dutch Selgado's rackets. She was sure of that. She had heard that Teddy wanted out, but no one just quit Selgado. Unless it was feet first.

"Did they try to sell forged paintings," I inquired.

"I don't know," was her answer.

They decided on Times Square for a movie.

While the women went to the ladies' room, Tom and I talked in the lobby. "Might just turn out to be a hit by someone who found out he bought a bag of wax," Tom said. "Teddy Noren's killing, anyway."

"But if Dutch had Teddy killed," I said, "then likewise with Bram Walker ..."

"Are we getting anywhere?"

"We know Dutch is behind the crack operation. Is he into forgeries? Does he use them to launder the money through Myra's art gallery? I don't think either one of us would be surprised. But why put the bite on Lloyd Henderson? No doubt Selgado's rackets are big money business. What in the world is 50 grand? And why Henderson?"

"You think Dutch framed Paul Manfred?"

"If he did, he had help. Sandra, I'll bet."

"Sandra sneaks the gun out of her old man's house, gives it to Dutch, and one of Dutch's boys eliminates Walker."

"It makes sense."

The two women joined us again, and we went to see the movie. Stella smelled of delicate perfume, I felt content, and we laughed when the funny lines were spoken. It was a comedy. At this point I needed some humor.

We dropped them home, called it a night and headed back.

❋❋❋

Tom and I got to the office on time for a change. Two messages for me. Or rather a phone number on each message. With just an initial. P.

I took the two slips of paper downstairs with me and used one of the phones in the lobby. I recognized Paul Manfred's voice. "Is it safe to talk?" he said.

"I'm in the lobby of my office building. No police with me."

"Henderson told me to call you."

"What do you want?"

"What do I want? I want out. I don't need this mess."

"Where do we meet?"

"How about Washington Square Park? Under the arch?"

"In an hour?"

"Sure." He hung up, and I hung up.

I decided not to go back up stairs. I called Hildy and told her to tell Tom to stay ready. Twenty minutes later I was in Washington Square Park, under the arch. I waited three or four minutes before Paul Manfred showed up. He was wearing a faded denim jacket with fringes, denim pants, and he needed a shave. He wore a Mets' cap and sun glasses. We strolled to a bench and sat down. The sun was out, and it looked like it was going to be nice for the rest of the day.

"Who put the police on me?" he asked.

"How should I know?"

"You didn't bring the cops, he said. "I've been watching you from Fifth Avenue. I can't trust anyone. Even old man Henderson. He won't even get me a lawyer. He just told me to talk to you."

"When did you see him?"

"I talked to him early this morning." Paul Manfred didn't look too good. There were dark lines under his eyes. "Rich old computer man and that's all he could do for me."

"You want to talk about it?"

"Sure. But I don't know who killed Bram Walker. I don't know how the killer got my gun."

"I can't believe that," I said.

"I have a couple of ideas. Sandra or the old man. Cora is out of it."

"You're sure?"

"She's what you would call a non-entity."

"You just said you didn't know how the killer got your gun. Now you mention Sandra and Lloyd Henderson."

"I still say it. The gun was in a locked briefcase, and I have the only key."

"So the gun was taken after the case was forced open," I supplied.

"The briefcase wasn't forced. But Sandra could have managed it. She could have used the key while I was sleeping."

"If that's how it was done, then that means this set-up was all planned in advance. But I can't see Sandra working on her own. What's behind all of this? I want to know. Two artists get knocked off. Somebody puts the bite on your boss for 50 grand. Marilyn Riley, the granddaughter, gets mixed up in some crack dealing racket. I find a forged painting. Where is the connection?"

"I've got the 50 gees," Paul Manfred said.

I almost fell off the park bench. "What! But—How did you get it away from Dutch? You hypnotize him or something?"

Paul grinned, but there was no humor in it. "Sandra and I worked the blackmail angle. I'm telling you this, but it doesn't go any further. I'll just deny every word."

"Okay," I said.

"Blackmail is one thing, but murder is something else. I won't be a patsy for Sandra, or Dutch."

"How does Dutch fit into this situation? What the heck is 50 grand to someone like Dutch?"

"Nothing. But 50 grand is 50 grand to someone like me. The old man paid me peanuts. Room and board. I wanted out and figured 50 grand would be more than enough pay for all the abuse I've taken from that vampire. Sandra helped me. It's not the money with her; she and Cora have it in for the old man. We knew about Marilyn and the cocaine. Sandra found out from Dutch. She put on a wig and went out with him for kicks. I think she has a few cards missing from her deck. It was Dutch's racket, and he thought it was funny that Marilyn was one of his street sellers, and Sandra was her aunt. So Sandra and I used that to put the squeeze on Henderson. Dutch went along with it. He would have one of his gofers take the dough from whoever delivered it, and then he would hand it over to me."

"Okay," I said, absorbing all this. "And Dutch helped out of the goodness of his heart?"

"No. We would owe him a favor. That was the way he put it."

"I cannot buy it the way it stands," I said. "You've got to be holding out."

"If it wasn't for the frame, I wouldn't be talking to you now."

"Why don't you go to the cops?"

"I have a record. And the blackmail deal. They would figure if I did blackmail, I would commit murder."

That made some sense. "The police can't see you killing Walker and then leaving your own gun behind. A registered gun. How did you get a gun license with your record?"

"Henderson pulled some strings," Paul said.

"What about the killings?"

"I'm out of that," he said. "Maybe it's a separate item. Nothing to do with the Hendersons."

"Maybe, and maybe not."

"Henderson told me to talk to you and I did. Can you help me?"

"Help you how?"

"I don't know. I'm hot right now. Maybe you can take the 50 grand off my hands?"

I grinned at him. "I'm not that stupid. All you have to do is tip off the police that I have the money, and I'm hooked for blackmail. Maybe the police will throw in a murder or two."

"You're not very trusting, are you?" Paul said quietly.

"I'm just not crazy. I never trust people who give me half a story. You're right in the mess up to your ears. Maybe you didn't murder anyone, but you know who's behind it all. I shouldn't even be talking to you."

"Maybe I need an ace in the hole."

"You're not holding any cards, pal. You want to go for a fall, that's your business."

He was sweating now, and he looked at me with eyes that were desperate. "Maybe I just have a crazy idea."

"How crazy?"

"You're an honest person, aren't you?"

I said nothing.

"I'm glad you didn't bring the law," he said, and started to walk away.

"What's behind it all?" I said to him loudly.

He heard me, and he kept on going. I stood up, and he walked under the arch and onto Fifth Avenue.

I sat on the bench and watched the drug dealers in action. Stroll up to a customer, reach in their own mouth and pull a rock of crack out from their cheek, haggle, and hand it over for $15, cash. Customer then stashes it his own mouth. Lost in the crowd. Great way to pass AIDS, I thought—never mind hepatitis. They carry it in their cheek because crack won't dissolve in saliva—and they can swallow the rock if cops start questioning them. How did the buyer know he wasn't getting a chunk of paraffin? Guess he just found out later. *Caveat emptor.* It was getting chilly, and I felt hungry. May was just a couple of days away.

I didn't want to eat. I just wanted to think. Manfred had been framed by someone who wanted him out of the way. He thought it was Sandra that had taken his gun. Had Sandra also shot Bram Walker? Had she also killed Teddy Noren?

How much truth was there in what Manfred had told me? Why didn't I get some food and give my mind a rest?

I found a Mexican restaurant on University Place and ate a beef enchilada with some chili and beans, and drank a large lemonade.

I called Hildy and told her I was going home and to tell Tom he could take off and do whatever he wanted.

The phone was ringing when I opened the door to my apartment. It was Myra. "Where have you been keeping yourself?" she said. "You don't work 24 hours a day, do you?"

"I'm training to become a social pariah."

"I can come over, and we'll train together," She coyed.

"I'm world weary. Accounting out. Not fit company for anyone."

"How about lunch tomorrow?"

"I'll have to call you."

"Have you heard anything about Paul?"

"Not a thing." I evaded.

"There was nothing in the papers."

"You want the papers to print that the police are still looking for him? That's not what they call news. When the police find him, there'll be an item in the papers. If the police prove he did the murders, then it'll be quite a story. Maybe make the headlines."

"Do you think Paul killed Bram and Teddy?" Her voice was sultry.

"I'm too tired to think. I just want to relax in front of my TV and watch a good movie."

"But it's so early."

"I'll call you tomorrow."

There was nothing worth watching on TV, and I poured myself a Coke, sat on my couch and just vegged-out for a while. I kept the Hendersons and the Rileys out of my brain.

I went to the bookshelf and found Coleridge:

> In Xanadu did Kubla Khan
> A stately pleasure-dome decree
> Where Alph, the sacred river, ran
> Through caverns measureless to man
> Down to a sunless sea.

I wasn't entirely a mug. There was nothing to do but to get some rest and start fresh tomorrow morning.

I put away Coleridge and took myself to the bathroom where I boiled for half an hour in my specially installed Jacuzzi and then went to bed. First I took the phone off the hook. If anyone wanted me they would have to kick down the front door. No one kicked down my front door.

I was thankful for that. Certainly they wouldn't find me in the great State of Texas, my next stop.

Twelve

Forensic accounting refers to the application of accounting principles, theories, and discipline to facts or hypotheses at issue in a legal dispute and encompasses every branch of accounting knowledge.
—AICPA's Management Advisory
Services Technical Consulting
Practice Aid 7: ***Litigation Services***

The flight to Fort Worth allowed me to continue my preparation for the courtroom battle tomorrow. Forensic accounting covers two broad areas: litigation support and investigative accounting. The AICPA describes litigation services as any professional assistance non-lawyers provide to lawyers in the litigation process. The Henderson case was allowing me to behave like an investigative accountant, though at times I felt I was acting more like a detective. Something that was not my primary objective. In most crimes, there's no doubt a crime has been committed. It's the criminal you're trying to identify. In a financial fraud, you usually know who the person is that's involved. What you are attempting to do is demonstrate that the actions taken were fraudulent in nature, that is, intentionally deceptive and injurious. The Henderson engagement had attributes of both, making it doubly complex.

Rick Mannino had sent me two newspaper articles from the ***Dallas Times Herald***. A reporter, Robert Deitz, had described the stereotypical image of an accountant: "After all, everyone knows that bean counters are bespectacled, pale-skinned wretches who spend mind-numbing lives in dreary cubicles poring over faint computer printouts and dusty ledgers. Right?"

Tomorrow I would be testifying in court for General Dynamics, providing litigation support. Working in concert with high-powered lawyers, and keeping a clear-headed, unemotional bearing under intensive cross examination. My job would be to provide credible expert opinion on complex accounting issues. The opposing attorney's job would be to make me look like a lying idiot. Any anger, loss of confidence, or other emotional lapse he can drive or insult me into, will inure to his purpose. My experience as a professor would work to my favor, since my career centers around explaining complex accounting issues in clear understandable terms.

What I need to guard against, is treating the jury like my students. The opposing lawyer will accuse me of grandstanding and thinking I'm back in my ivory tower. He'll try to make me look like a fool. The judge *owns* the courtroom. The witness is just a guest—and one that not every party appreciates.

Nevertheless, I liked the grueling task of preparing beforehand and participating in a courtroom battle over accounting principles. There was the challenge to react and respond to the many innuendoes and leading questions asked by the opposing attorney. Probably the stress was not worth the daily fees I received, but I kind of enjoyed it. I sometimes imagined the opposing attorney to be a black-clad medieval knight racing toward me on horseback with a long, sharp lance. I always toppled the vicious knight in my daydreams. Though not always in court.

The other Dallas newspaper article by John A. Bolt gave the reason for forensic accountants:

> Robbers do not need guns. Pencil and paper will do. Opportunity and greed are thievery's driving forces. Put enough zeroes behind a number, and it's amazing how flexible morals become. How many years in prison would you do to accumulate a half a billion dollars in your bank account?

I took a taxi to the Westin Hotel, in the Galleria, off LBJ Freeway at the Dallas Parkway. Inside my room, I picked up the Guest Informant. An article by A.D. Greene described Dallas from the air:

> The country under the jet's wing is green, not brown; the landscape is dotted with lakes large and small, so many they look like various-sized bits of broken mirror scattered about the landscape.

I turned on the television and saw David Letterman list his top reasons for being an accountant:

- CPAs always have lead in their pencils.
- Old accountants never die, they just lose their balance.
- Accountants are calculating.
- Ticking comes naturally to accountants.
- Accountants: the few, the proud, the boss.
- Accountant's reversing entry: 00.8 Taxes.

Later Bob Newhart, a former accountant, came on to promote his new movie: Naked Gun 357.

❖❖❖

"Professor Cramer, for the court's record, please state your full name and current address."

"Paul Leonard Cramer, the third, 1250 Liberty Court, New York, New York."

"Dr. Cramer, we wish to thank you for testifying today as an expert witness about certain accounting matters. First, I have several questions for you concerning your background. Where did you obtain you Ph.D. degree?"

"University of Illinois."

"Where did you receive your MBA degree?"

"Harvard University."

"Where did you receive your bachelor's degree?"

"Amherst."

"Are you listed in Who's Who in America?"
"Yes."
"What years were you president of the American Accounting Association?"
"That was 1989-90."

I had rehearsed most of these questions and answers the night before.

"Professor Cramer, have you written any accounting books?"
"I have written four accounting books. Two cost accounting textbooks, a forensic accounting book, plus an accounting casebook for MBA students."
"Would you please explain what is meant by forensic accounting?"
"Briefly, forensic accounting is a science that deals with the relation and application of accounting facts to business and social problems." I smiled and turned toward the jury. "As I tell my students, a forensic accountant is like the Columbo or Quincy characters of yesteryear, except he or she uses accounting records and facts to uncover fraud, missing assets, insider tradings and other white-collar crimes." I turned back to the pinstriped lawyer.

"Dr. Cramer, where are you currently employed?"
"I am the Sidney Paton Professor of Accounting at Columbia University."
"Is it an honor to hold a professorship?"
"Yes, there are few professorships in accounting." I thought, yes, no money, just a title. The real money is in a 'chair' designation. I was still searching for a chair designation at an agreeable university.

"Professor Cramer, are you a Certified Public Accountant?"
"Yes, in Pennsylvania, since 1970," I responded.
"Are you a member of the American Institute of CPAs?"
"Yes, since 1970."
"Do you serve on the Board of Directors of any major corporations?"
"Yes, I serve on the Board of Directors of four of the top Fortune one hundred companies and for three smaller companies."

"Dr. Cramer, are you an outside consultant?"
"Yes."
"Please estimate how many professional articles you have written."
"About 70." I shifted in the wooden chair.
"Uh." The attorney shuffled several pages and then continued, "have you ever appeared as an expert witness in the courtroom?"
"Yes. I have been an expert witness for accounting matters on about 11 different occasions—two oil companies, two banks, one insurance company, a manufacturing company, an accounting firm, the Internal Revenue Service, the SEC, and two divorce cases."

The attorney turned to the judge and said, "Your honor, we present to this court Dr. Cramer, as an expert witness in the area of forensic accounting."

The robed judge turned to the opposing attorney and said, "Mr. Fletcher, do you have any objections to this request?"

Attorney Fletcher stood up and spoke loudly, "No, your honor."

"So moved. You may proceed, counselor."

"Dr. Cramer, what type of cost is the security service with General Dynamics. The approximately $2 million expense for security guards."

"These costs would be classified as indirect costs. According to the Federal Acquisition Regulations, an indirect cost is one not directly identified with a single, final cost objective, but identified with two or more final cost objectives or an intermediate cost objective."

"Professor, what should be done with these indirect costs?" the attorney for G.D.C. asked.

"These indirect costs, such as the security expenses, should be accumulated by logical cost groupings with due consideration of the reason for incurring the expenditures. Since these indirect overhead costs are common to more than one department, they should be shared. Each department should be charged with its fair share of these security costs."

"Now Professor Cramer, how are these costs shared with the various departments?"

"Obviously these costs must be allocated to the various departments with a reasonable allocation base. This allocation base must be fair and equitable. Think of it as a cost driver—an activity or procedure that causes costs to be incurred."

"What would be a good cost driver for these security costs, Dr. Cramer?" The attorney smiled slightly.

I shifted in the hard seat and then replied. "These costs are general and administrative expenses. Similar to personnel costs, I believe they could be allocated based upon either number of employees, labor hours, or labor costs."

"Who should determine how costs should be allocated: the government or the contractor?"

"I believe that cost allocation should be the function of the contractor, not the government. The selection of an accounting system is the responsibility and prerogative of management—*as long as* the procedure follows generally accepted accounting principles."

"How does General Dynamics allocate these costs?"

"By total direct engineering labor hours."

"Does this meet generally accepted accounting practice?"

"Yes, it does," I replied.

✦✦✦

The attorneys each acted in the role of opposing movie directors—calling witnesses and orchestrating carefully timed presentations. All of it designed to sway the jury's disposition in favor of their respective clients position. Civil cases, like this one, are decided based only on which side has the greatest preponderance of evidence in it's favor. Evidence of guilt or innocence beyond a reasonable doubt is the criterion for deciding criminal cases only, and therefore did not apply to this case. It turned out my role was relatively small in this case, but the *per diem* fees were nonetheless quite substantial.

I had some time before my plane flight back to New York, so I walked from my room in the Westin Hotel at the Galleria, to the lobby. Several people were walking around with COPAS name-tags: Council of Petroleum Accountants Societies. There was a seminar in the hotel for oil and gas instructors sponsored by COPAS and the University of North Texas.

As I started walking into the Galleria, I passed a Gallery of History store. Inside I saw a 1948 baseball signed by Jackie Robinson—$4,299. There was a red boxing glove signed by Larry Holmes, priced at $899.

Many of the historical items were business-related. Lottery ticket number 120 was signed by George Washington in 1768: $22,000. The display indicated that in Colonial times, lotteries were a popular way to raise funds for roads in Virginia, Maryland, and Pennsylvania. Have we come full circle?

A canceled check for $8.04, signed in 1928 by Thomas A. Edison now sold for $2,000. A Rick Nelson check for $3,799, signed in 1985 now sold for $4,000. A $28.05 canceled check signed by Orville Wright in 1945 was priced at $1,200. Amazing.

"Hello, may I help you? I'm Tim Proudfoot."

"I bet many people ask you if you're an Indian," I said.

"Yes. Actually I'm Irish."

After talking with Tim for sometime, he told me that in college he had a full-blooded Indian friend named Riley. They had a lot fun with the two ethnic names.

"We bring history alive," was Tim's description of the purpose of the gallery.

Continuing my stroll around the gallery, I saw a manuscript letter signed by George Washington in 1798 priced at $65,000. The Challenger Astronauts photo with signatures on envelopes, $19,000. A signed photo of Adolf 'Der Fuhrer' Hitler, $13,000.

My favorite was a Geronimo photograph. His signature was printed in large letters—not signed. $35,000. The Human Tiger was called the greatest General that ever lived by U.S. Senator Foraker.

I almost purchased a baseball signed by the eight living pitchers who had pitched a perfect game. My favorite Dodger, Sandy Koufax, was one of the pitchers. Instead, I purchased a book.

In the center of the Galleria was an ice rink. Mostly young children with white, green, orange, or black skates went round and round the rink. There were three cascading light chandeliers rising to the glass ceiling. They were about three stories tall.

There were real, green trees around the rink and the food court. After an enchilada dinner at the El Fenix Café, I took a taxi to the airport. I saw a bumper sticker on a Chevrolet as we left the parking lot: "I ♥ MY CPA."

On my flight back to New York, I read ***Collecting Historical Documents: A Guide to Owning History***, by Todd M. Axelrod. One autograph letter dated August 13, 1941, signed by "Old Blood and Guts" George S. Patton, Jr. caught my attention. In a letter to the headmaster at his son's school, Patton said about his son: "George is a poor student—possibly stupid." I wondered if the kid grew up feeling very confident.

I picked up the ***Wall Street Journal***—southwest edition—and a Section B article on the prices at a recent Sotheby's Holding, Inc. auction caught my attention. Among other items it listed the sale of a three-dimensional painting in soft folded lead by modern artist Jannis Kounellis. Kounellis ... Kounellis ... I hurriedly opened my briefcase and pulled out the list of paintings sold by Myra's art gallery. There it was. The very same painting. Sold in the same month. But a month is a lot of time.

Thirteen

Get this in your head. There is only one indicator for telling the value of paintings, and that is in the salesroom.

—Renior

I showed Hildy the **Wall Street Journal** article I'd seen on the plane from Dallas. Asked her to contact Sotheby's and see if they would fax us any info they had on the Kounellis painting: dates, prices, history of previous ownership—anything they had.

I skipped breakfast and Hildy sent out for coffee. Tom was in and I sent for him. When it arrived, he helped himself to some of my coffee.

I told him about my conversation with Paul Manfred before my trip to Texas.

"You should have grabbed him," Tom said.

"Where would that get me? He would only clam up."

"At least now you know it was Manfred and Sandra who masterminded the great 50 grand blackmail racket."

"Yes. Fifty thousand. Sandra has a lot more to lose if she's caught."

"And don't forget our pal Dutch," Tom said. He was perched on the edge of my desk. "So now Paul owes him a favor. What sort of favor?"

"He didn't say. Maybe something Dutch had in mind and was hoping Paul would play ball—or maybe take a fall," I speculated.

"We're nowhere."

"Paul Manfred didn't seem that worried for a guy who has a flock of cops looking for him."

"And Manfred said something about an ace in the hole?" Tom mused. "I think Manfred gave you a song and dance about just wanting 50 grand. A red herring."

"Maybe."

"You think Henderson will go to bat for him?"

"Manfred doesn't think so," I informed Tom. "He seems pretty bitter about Lloyd Henderson."

"Could be an act."

"Listen, Tom, I can't go around carrying a lie detector with me. It would be a great thing if everyone told me the truth. But to some people, lying is second nature."

"Now for the good news. I found some evidence that at least one of the paintings sold by Myra's art gallery had to be a fake." I told Tom about the sale of the Kounellis painting at Sotheby's auction, and that it was on the gallery's sales list he had given me.

Hildy poked her head in. "There's a Frank Masters to see you."

I told Tom to duck out and check into the local buyer of the Kounellis painting from Myra's gallery—to see if the buyer was also a fake.

Hildy showed Masters to my office. He was dressed in a navy-blue blazer and beige cotton pants, open collar shirt and cordovan penny loafers. No pennies in the loafers. As he sat down, he looked nervous and his hands trembled. I didn't think it was an act. He looked like a frightened man.

"I've been threatened," the artist said.

"By whom?"

"I—I don't know."

He saw my skeptical look and wrung his hands even more. "What difference does it make? I can't go to the police. I don't know what to do."

"You can't go to the police because of the racket you're in?" I said.

"There's no use pretending, is there?"

"I'm an accountant. Why are you coming to me?"

"I need help. I'm willing to pay."

"I'm not a bodyguard."

"Look, Dr. Cramer, I didn't know how deep I was getting into this mess. That's the truth. The crack dealing—well, I had no idea it was going to end up with people getting murdered. I knew I was in bad company but—." He started to chew his lip.

"Dutch Selgado is bad company."

"Crack is just a sideline to him," Masters said.

"I guess you know about as much as I do."

"Yes. Dutch. He has his fingers in a lot of rackets. Then Teddy gets killed, then Bram. I had a funny feeling I was slated to be next. Then—"

"Then what?"

"Princess came to see me. She works for Selgado and recruits the girls as street dealers. She said it would be better for everyone if I took a long vacation. She said she was telling me as a favor to Nadja. Nadja liked me. I haven't see her for a couple of days. The Princess looked at me as if I was a dead man. Then later when I went to a cafe for a late breakfast, a car came from nowhere, tried to run me down. I didn't know where else to go, so I came to you."

"Who took the scales out of Teddy Noren's apartment?" I asked.

"I did."

"Who killed him?"

"I don't know. Really. It wasn't Bram. He wouldn't have killed anyone. And I know I didn't."

"Something has been eating me up," I said. "I found a canvas in Teddy Noren's apartment. An oil. Teddy used acrylic. Why should the killer shoot Noren and then waste time painting a picture?"

"That painting has nothing to do with Teddy's death," Masters said.

"How do you know?"

"Look, Teddy painted that picture in acrylic. I went over it with oil."

Answers. It's wonderful.

"Some artists do it that way. They do a painting in acrylic and then go over it with oil. We did that lots of times. I was with Teddy in his apartment. I had my oils with me. In a case. He put the canvas on the easel and asked me to go over it with oil. That's what I did. Then I left. When I found out Teddy was dead, I didn't want to be implicated. So I kept my mouth shut about being there.

You can have an expert check that canvas. Under the oil painting you'll find acrylic."

"Why didn't Teddy do it himself?"

"He didn't like working with oils. He felt it wasn't his medium. What difference does it make anyway?"

"None, I guess, except it was a forgery."

"Hey, I just put oil over the acrylic. Copying famous paintings is good exercise."

So that was finally out of the way. I believed Masters. It was easy enough to check it out by having someone look at the painting. But why bother at this point? It made sense. Masters knew it could be checked. Maybe he never even knew that Teddy and Marilyn were probably using the paintings to cover up drug proceeds for Dutch Selgado. But did that leave him off the hook? He could still have killed Noren after going over the canvas with oil. But what would be his motive?

"Are you going to help me?" Masters said.

"Your only recourse is to go the police."

"And go to jail."

"They might actually believe you."

Masters got up and walked to the window and looked out at the Chrysler Building.

"It looks like Dutch is cleaning out this operation," I said to his back. "You're a witness. You know too much. If you want to save your hide, you should get out quickly."

Masters turned to me. "Do you think he killed Teddy and Bram?"

"It isn't exactly a gangster's style—shooting someone and leaving the gun behind to make it look like suicide."

"Teddy didn't have an enemy in the world," Masters said. "There were a few people who didn't like Bram, but not bad enough to kill him."

"I don't have the answers."

Masters rubbed the knuckles of his right fist against his teeth. "I can't just leave everything behind."

He was still undecided. Everything had snowballed into a deadly nightmare. He couldn't fight gangsters. If he went to the police, he would end up in prison. Better that than dead.

Then he nodded at me slowly and went to the door and out. I watched him go. One more lost soul.

The woods were full of lost souls.

I was knee deep in lost souls. Good old Marilyn. I hadn't seen Marilyn for a while. What was she up to?

It wasn't long when Myra called.

How about lunch?

Sure. I would love to have lunch.

We would meet in Herald Square in the small park and figure out where to go.

I told Hildy I was going out for lunch and would be back in a couple of hours.

Myra Riley was dressed in a white knit suit, and she looked out of place next to the seedy characters in the small park. There was the usual traffic jam in front of Macy's. I sat down on the bench beside her. She took my hand and gave it a squeeze. "Well I hope you're not avoiding me," she said.

"I've been rather busy. Had to fly to Fort Worth. Trying to put the pieces together. Too many pieces, Myra."

"When the police catch Paul ..."

"You think that will end it?" I said. "Come on, Myra. Don't be naive. Paul is just one small piece in this crazy puzzle."

She looked at a loss, and I didn't bother to explain further. She could have been acting, or she knew something, or everything, and I would be wasting my time. I didn't know much, but something was afoot, as my grand uncle Sherlock Holmes used to say.

We found an English style steak house and had thin sliced beef on rye bread. I drank a Dr. Pepper, remembering the sign in Arlington Stadium. "Have you seen Marilyn lately?" I asked.

"Yesterday."

"What's she doing?"

"Nothing now."

The gravy was spicy. I ran a piece of beef around in it and munched it.

"Do you want to talk to Marilyn?" she asked.

"Now where would that get me?"

"You think Marilyn is evasive?"

"As much as anyone in this engagement is." I watched her drink and wondered how innocent she was. I didn't think she killed the artists. I was pretty sure Dutch didn't. But Dutch could have tried to run down Frank Masters—if he was clearing out the operation. Maybe he was scared of the heat, or he was into something really big. I had the feeling he was into something big.

"Did your father ever talk to you about this microchip of his? Something about a new kind of memory? A new kind of high-powered computer? Anything?"

"Are you kidding? We don't talk; we don't even see each other. And when I was living at the house, he never talked to us about his business."

"He doesn't have anything valuable in his house or in a vault? A diamond or a ruby."

"No. He doesn't collect anything now except paintings."

"Now who mentioned painting to me? I think it was Sandra. Yes."

"The prize is, of course, the Turner."

"The English painter?"

"Yes. But his painting is locked up in a special room. You need a special key and there are alarms."

"Turner? Maybe that's the McGuffey Sandra mentioned."

"The thing everybody wants. Like in the Hitchcock movies."

"That's right," I said guardedly.

"There's Picasso, Braque ..."

"Are they real? Any forgeries?"

She appeared shocked. "He only bought originals."

"Finish your drink, and let's get out of here."

West 57th Street was loaded with art galleries. Not the shlock chain-store galleries. Here was the real thing. If you had the facts and figures, that is. Henri Matisse, John Singer Sargent, Winslow Homer, Klimt, Kokoschka. We selected the first one we found and the clerk was prissy and probably wondered if we had lost our way. Then Myra described the Turner and his face glowed as if he was plugged into a neutron reactor.

And while the clerk gushed with his face, I was admiring a Remmington. I had discovered Texas sunsets really do look like that. "How much would that Turner be worth?" I asked the clerk when Myra had finished.

"Well, one sold about two years ago for about three million dollars," the clerk said. "My name is Alexander Peers." He handed me a business card.

"It would have to go up for auction to get the right price, I take it? Mr. Peers."

"Oh, of course."

"What about a stolen one?"

"Stolen?" He was indignant. "No reputable dealer would touch it. Only an unscrupulous private collector, who would never exhibit it."

"But there are such collectors?"

"Unfortunately, yes," the clerk said. "Paintings, stamps, and coins. One stolen Brasher Doubloon worth a half-million dollars has never turned up. In the hands of a dishonest private collector, I suppose."

"What would the price be for a Turner?"

"That's very difficult to say. There are so many factors in that type of situation. A Turner. Three million, I would guess. Possibly four. You know the art market crashed in the late eighties. Prices for some impressionist paintings tumbled as much as 50 percent from the art market's peak in 1989. But the market turned the corner in 1992, and now is the time to buy. Why in May, 1992, Braque's Cubist masterwork 'Atelier VII' sold for $7.7 million."

I ignored the sales pitch. "And if the Turner went up for auction?"

"Oh, much more now. Not many Turners come up for auction. The museums never give them up. And the collectors who have them would never sell unless they were experiencing serious financial, uh ... embarrassment."

I took Myra's hand, thanked the clerk, and we left.

"You must be wrong," Myra said outside, on the sidewalk, with a grinning sun overhead. "No one can get anywhere near that Turner. It would be like breaking into a vault."

"Vaults have been broken into before."

"But who?"

"Cora. Sandra."

"Certainly not Cora. She's content with what she has, believe me. And Sandra—she has what she wants."

"Are you sure about that?"

"She won't go against my father. That would be stupid. She would be cut out of his will. She's his daughter, not his wife. In this state a wife can't be disinherited. If she is, she still gets a fourth of the estate. No, Sandra wouldn't antagonize our father."

"For two or three million, I think she'd take a chance. She'd really be independent from him. I wonder if the Turner painting has been donated to Columbia University."

"What are you talking about."

"Oh, that's the reason I'm involved in this mess. Henderson has donated some of his art collection to Columbia University. My president asked me—uh, bent my elbow—to help Henderson."

"He probably did not give the Turner away," I said almost to myself. "In a charitable remainder trust, the donor irrevocably gives up the asset, takes a tax deduction based upon the age of the donor, and gets income for life."

"Why would my father need income for life?"

"I don't know. Maybe he had cash flow problems. For someone with highly appreciated assets, a charitable remainder trust is a great way to improve cash flow and make a charitable gift at the same time. But you do give up the asset—the painting."

We started walking towards Fifth Avenue. "If Sandra did get the Turner," Myra said, "How would she get rid of it? She would need a private collector; one who wouldn't care if he exhibited the painting or not; one who would buy a stolen painting."

"Who comes in contact with collectors? Artists."

"And art galleries."

I calmly asked her about the three-dimensional painting by Jannis Kounellis. As best she could remember, Marilyn had sold the painting to a customer for about $180,000. I did not press the issue.

We had a pleasant walk in the park, and then we agreed to dinner. I put her in a cab. She gave me a warm smile. Pretty eyes. I felt myself lean forward, touch her hair and kiss her gently. I shut the door for her and strolled to Park Avenue.

At a phone booth I called my office. Hildy told me nothing was stirring. Sotheby's had agreed to fax us a copy of their auction prospectus, along with some other info, and she was waiting on its arrival. I hung up and took a bus to 42nd Street, got an add-a-ride, took the cross-town and went up to the office.

Tom was there, and I brought him into my office and told him what I thought.

"Fake paintings being used to launder drug money," he said. "Could be we're making some progress. I looked for the purchaser of the Kounellis painting—fake all right. The address was an abandoned warehouse building in Queens. Not as exotic as a blood red ruby. Something called the Star of Asia."

"You can't have everything."

"We don't live right. A missing ruby, a chase through a moving train, corpses in every compartment—that's a life for Sherlock Holmes. So what do we get? Gangster killings and money laundering."

"Hold on. What's this about gangster killings?"

"That's my conclusion, Lenny. I've been thinking and thinking and can't see anything else. Dutch ordered the killings. Had it set up so it would look like suicides so the cops won't think gangsters did it. This scenario leads the police away from old Dutch Selgado."

It did make some sense the way Tom put it, but I just couldn't buy the theory. "And motive?" I said.

"Maybe Dutch is a member of the Kill An Artist a Month Club," Tom speculated.

"So you don't have a motive?"

"How about clearing up the operation. Maybe he doesn't want the racket."

"So he kills two artists who are trying to get out and know too much, who also paint the imitations, but only warns off the third." I told Tom about Frank Masters and the attempt on his life.

"You can't say things aren't coming to a head."

"You track down some more of the purchasers of the paintings sold by Marilyn. One misplaced customer isn't going to be enough evidence. I want to see Marilyn."

Marilyn Riley was home, polishing her toe nails. She had on shorts and a gray sweatshirt with "Shop Till You Drop" across the front, with one foot on a hassock. Cranberry colored polish.

"What now?"

"Did Teddy know any art collectors?"

"Of course. Who do you think bought his paintings, hardware salesmen?"

"Did he know any rich art collectors? The ones who go for Picasso and Winslow?"

"No, of course not. They wouldn't bother with someone like Teddy. They wouldn't even go to art exhibits in the Village or 59th Street. Those babies go to 57th Street. The real posh places."

"What about Walker and Masters?"

"I doubt it."

I watched her dab at a toenail with a little brush. "Have you heard from the Princess or Nadja?"

"You know about the Princess, huh? No, I haven't heard from either of them."

The phone rang and it was Hildy. "Mr. Henderson just called. He's in his office, and he wants you to call him pronto."

And I did. "Where are you?" Henderson said.

I told him. He wanted the address, and I gave it to him.

"You will wait for me outside. I will pick you up shortly. We will proceed to my home."

"Sure. What's up?"

"Someone has broken into my home." He sounded as if he was announcing a stock quotation. "One of my paintings has been stolen. My pride and joy."

"The Turner?"

"Yes. How did you know?"

"That was obvious, Mr. Henderson. It was your favorite."

The black Fleetwood stretch limousine sped smoothly away from Soho. I sat in the back with Lloyd Henderson. "Sandra called me half an hour ago. She was rather incoherent. She and the household staff were bound and gagged. The thieves broke into the room where my paintings hang. The alarms went off, of course. They worked like fiends. They took the Turner before the police arrived. The police freed everyone, and Sandra called me. And I called you. I'm impressed with the way it was done, but that was my property, Dr. Cramer, and I want it back." He demanded.

"Where was Cora all this time?"

"She was also tied up. Didn't I mention her? Well, Cora blends so with the background sometimes I forget she's around."

"I'm sure she appreciates that."

"Cora is like an inanimate object. You see her but feel nothing."

"She moves, breathes, and has feelings. Just like the rest of us."

"Don't concern yourself with Cora, Doctor. When I die she will be a rich woman. I doubt she will travel any or enjoy life. She is part of my house. She will not leave it. She is—uh—conditioned. She's like an android. She is deaf, dumb, and blind. She is one of the roses in my garden. She is one of the trees on my property. She is a piece of furniture."

So much for fatherhood. We weren't going by train. We were going straight through by car. And we broke the speed limits. Surprisingly on the L.I.E. we got away with it. Mr. Henderson was in a hurry to see the damage. If he was seething inside, he didn't show it much.

What makes the Hendersons of the world? Greed, I guess. Baby seals were bludgeoned with clubs in Canada so that West German sophisticates could wear their soft furs. It came under the heading of greed. Stone cold greed.

Henderson loved possessions and used people—even his own family, and now he was getting the dirty end of the stick. There was silence in the car now, heavy, perfumed with deep thoughts. A gang had pulled off the robbery. Primed and timed. That meant only one thing—Dutch Selgado.

I thought I now knew why the artists had been killed. It was all connected. It had to be.

The place was swarming with Long Beach police. In the big front room the household staff were being questioned by detectives, and fingerprint men were everywhere. I followed Henderson into the special room where his paintings were hanging on walls. There was a fortune there. Why didn't the thieves take everything? They took only his pride and joy.

One empty frame. The canvas had been taken from the frame and evidently rolled up. The Turner. Just rolled up and taken away.

A detective joined us. His name was Cyrus Balaban, first grade. He was tall and thin, his face was angular, and he wore a plain gray suit and a grim expression. From what he could gather from Cora, Sandra, and the servants, there had been four or five people involved in the theft. They had all worn stockings over their heads. No one had heard a car drive up, but after they had been bound and gagged and the painting taken, they had all heard at least two cars driving away. There could have been a third car. No wonder Balaban had a grim expression on his face. So far all the fingerprints found were from the servants and the sisters. But they couldn't account for one set, and they wanted to take Henderson's prints for comparison. He obligingly went away with Balaban.

I moved from painting to painting, knowing I would never again see such an array of masterpieces. An Henri Matisse. An early Picasso. I came across three German expressionists, Erich Heckel, Ernst Ludwig Kirchner and August Macke. The Macke showed a woman admiring a parrot in a shop window.

"Quite a collection, isn't it?" a controlled, feminine voice said.

She must walk like a cat, I thought as I turned around. There was a slight resemblance to Sandra as I faced Cora

Henderson. She wore a simple dress with puffed sleeves.

"Do you know anything about art?" I asked.

"Something. Not much. I do know my father loves these paintings. More than ..."

"More than his daughters?" I said.

"I believe so," she said hesitating, her face stiff.

"The thieves must have worked awfully fast."

"Yes. Like lightning." Her meticulously shaped eyebrows lifted slightly.

"Don't you need a special key to get into this room?"

"Yes. They must have had one. They couldn't have broken down the door. I don't know how they got a key."

"Where did your father keep the key?"

"In his study, I believe."

"Easy enough for someone to borrow the key, have an impression made, put back the original key, and have one made from the impression."

"I don't know anything about such matters Dr. Cramer," she said, and left the room. I was left alone with paintings I would never own myself. Paintings that some collectors would almost be willing to give their souls to own. Not a very good bargain.

They could have taken the entire collection, but they didn't. Just one. A Turner. The owner's pride and joy. I knew a coin collector who owned rare coins, who valued them all, but treasured one more than all the others. And it wasn't the most expensive coin in his collection. A Romanian pattern, which hadn't even cost him much. The Turner was the prize in Henderson's collection, and I imagine it was because it was the most expensive—not much sentiment in Henderson.

Had the Turner been taken because it was the most valuable on the black market, or because it meant more to Henderson than all the others? That was something to think about. A psychological vendetta? Maybe.

I wandered absently out to the back porch, sat down, and watched a weary moon. Someone came up on the porch and stood quietly beside me for a moment. It was Sandra. I could smell her perfume.

"Some detective is coming out from Manhattan," she stated. "A specialist in stolen art. Everybody wants to get in on the act."

"There's already too many people in this act," I said. Some fog rolled in from the Sound, as hazy as gauze, with texture to it, leaving the skin of my face moist.

"Your mind must be working overtime," Sandra said.

"It's about time."

"You think you have it figured out?" Her voice was mocking.

"Some missing pieces. Everything will fall into place. King Lear and his three daughters."

"Goneril, Cordelia and Regan?"

"Cora, Sandra and Myra," I said.

How did a stolen, genuine masterpiece fit with the money laundering scheme using fakes? My mind wrestled. The fog was heavier now, and I could hardly see her. Then I didn't see her, she had retreated into the house. And I was alone, in the fog.

Fourteen

In summary, each cost center needs:

1. *A clear definition of its boundaries,*
2. *An estimate of the time period to accomplish measurable units of output, and*
3. *An understanding of the cost drivers that explain variation in costs (if any) with variation in the activity level in the cost center.*
   —H. Thomas Johnson and Robert S. Kaplan

He was a New York City detective, and he specialized in rare paintings. His name was Richard Steele, and he gave me a lift back to New York. The headlights reflected back blindingly in the fog; it was arduous driving.

"Joseph Mallord William Turner," the silver-haired detective said. "exhibited his first oil painting in 1799. He began his first impressionist style about 1830, both as to form and color. Some of his famous paintings are Kilchurn Castle, Lock Awe, The Wreck of the Minotaur, The Tenth Plague of Egypt. Lloyd Henderson's stolen painting was called Salvage at Sea. Quite a provenance. Some tin magnate bought it from a French duke, then sold it to one of the big galleries. Henderson acquired it at an auction. Paid just a bit over a million for it. Worth now maybe three or four million."

"Impressionists, along with contemporary paintings, have increased twice as fast as Old Masters, according to figures by Sotheby. More than securities," I said thinking back to the ***Wall Street Journal*** article I had read.

"So you know paintings. Paintings do *not* pay dividends like securities, however. Art can be stolen."

"Yasuda Fire & Marine apparently charged visitors $30 a visit to look at van Gogh's 'Sunflowers,' which was acquired in 1987 for $39.9 million," I replied. "Similar to dividends."

Steele didn't reply. He seemed to be thinking.

"What do you think the thieves will do with it?" I asked him.

"They may try to sell it back to Henderson through a go-between, or sell it to a collector who'll stick it away in some secret place and every now and then look at it and lick his lips and think he's on top of the world. His closest friends won't even know he has it. He couldn't take that kind of a chance."

"I've been hearing about such collectors," I said.

"Oh, they exist, all right."

"Don't you wonder why the thieves didn't take the whole collection?"

"It did cross my mind," he admitted. "There's one explanation. Some collector had heard about Henderson's Turner and wanted it. He got to the right people, and now he's the gloating possessor of a Turner. The thieves received the order and swiped only the painting this collector wanted. Simple, isn't it?"

"Yeah."

"You don't buy it, do you?"

I glanced at his profile. "No. Do you?"

"It's one explanation," he said. "Look, there are thieves who specialize in cars. They get an order for a particular car, so they go out and steal one. They bring it to their shop, and in hours the car gets chopped and re-identified. We just recently broke up an operation like that. That doesn't mean some other gang won't set up the same thing. As long as there's money in it, you'll find the crooks."

"They had to get a key," I said.

"Sure. So it was an inside job. One of the servants, probably. They're all being checked. If they find one with a record, he'll be watched, questioned, and so on."

We were in Manhattan, and he offered to drop me off at my apartment. I gave him my address. We were silent until he parked in front of my apartment building. "We may hit pay dirt and get them," he said.

"Look, I know I'm not going to be able to rest much. You want to come up for some coffee before going on in this fog?"

"Thanks."

Upstairs, I made some black coffee, and we sat at the dinette table and drank it. He looked at some stuff on the walls and said I had impressive taste. I said thanks, and then I laid the story out for him. Lloyd Henderson and his three daughters. The one who was cast adrift and the two who stayed.

Steele was about 50, slim, well dressed. Almost sophisticated, for a detective. "You think one of the daughters was the inside person?"

"I think so."

"Which one?"

I just shrugged and refilled the cups.

"If one of the daughters leaves the old man and suddenly starts throwing money around we'll have her."

"There's nerve and intelligence behind this robbery," I said. "If one of the daughters was behind it, she isn't going to give the show away. Unless she takes a trip to South America or Europe and starts living like a queen. And then you'll have to find the painting for your proof."

Steele made a fist, touched the first knuckle of his thumb to his upper lip. His brow intense. "We still haven't found Manfred. You think he was mixed up in the robbery?"

"I don't know. I think he knew it was coming."

"You haven't told me everything, have you?"

"Everything—except one thing that could get me into trouble."

He laughed at that. He relaxed his intent thoughts and drank some more coffee. "Why were the artists killed?"

"I think they knew what was going to happen," I said. "The robbery. The big one. I think somebody got high or careless and let it slip. I told you about Dutch. Dutch didn't kill the two artists. At least, I don't think he did. But he did try to scare Masters out of town—I'm pretty sure about that one."

"Wouldn't it be funny if Henderson was behind all this himself?" Steele said seriously. "He still keeps the painting, and collects $4,000,000 from his insurance company?" Steele said.

"That's been in my head too. Henderson has plenty of dough. But he's probably just greedy enough to try it. I don't know, somehow I think I'll rule him out for now."

"Is there anyone else you want to rule out?" Steele asked. I couldn't tell if he was being sarcastic, or just condescending.

"No."

"You think Dutch led those thieves today?"

"I think they were his men."

"And all we need is the proof."

"You may get it," I said. "Then again you may not. Let's hope they start fighting among themselves over the whole operation."

"That's a viable possibility, all right," Steele said. "But once thieves fall out, there's liable to be more shooting."

I didn't have anything to say to that.

I took the phone off the hook after Steele left. I didn't want to be disturbed by anyone. If the world came to an end, I didn't want to hear about it. I just wanted to zip myself into a vacuum and fade into warm restful slumber.

The morning was bright with sunshine. I called Tom at his apartment and told him to pick me up. I was downstairs when he showed up in a cab. We had the driver take us to Frank Masters' place.

We went to his apartment, and it was apparent that he had left in a real hurry. Tom used one of his special keys to get into the apartment. In the kitchen we made some coffee.

Tom knew about the stolen Turner; it had been on TV last night. "Everything was leading up to that, is that it?" he said. He sipped the coffee and made a face. He dumped it into the sink.

"I would say so."

"Can you tell me why we came here?"

"To see if Masters was really gone. I guess he did take off after all. Let's get out of here."

"You didn't finish your coffee."

We left and went to the accounting office.

John Grant was waiting for me. I sat in front of his desk and listened to him, and wished I had stayed in bed.

"I have police coming out of my ears," he bellowed. "And I had Henderson on the phone. He claims he hasn't gotten one thing out of us for his money. This an important client, and we can sell him on more accounting work if we come through on this engagement for him. He wants that expensive painting back. I told him we were the best people in New York, and if anyone could run it down and get it back, it's us. Now look, Lenny, you must have some ideas."

"Where is Henderson now?"

"In his New York office. Why?"

"Business as usual." I replied.

"What do you want him to do, stay home and bite his nails?"

"Yeah. Working keeps your mind off things."

"I know you'll come up with something, Lenny. You won't let me down. I'm confident of that."

"Right." I feigned.

I went to my own office and sat down behind my desk and thought about what next. What moves did I have open anyway?

Tom dropped in and said he'd bring up some decent coffee if I wanted it. I told him I'd wait for lunch.

Some police arrived at the office and asked a lot of routine questions. I was courteous and told them what they needed. They finally left, not terribly happy. I worked on a stale research project. **Management Accounting** had rejected one of my research papers.

Tom and I had lunch. Grilled steaks, baked potatoes with butter, sour cream and chives, house salads and iced tea. We sat in the back and watched a redhead toy with her food. When a man in a dark charcoal-gray business suit showed up, she seemed to brighten up and became more animated.

"I wish I had a redhead like that waiting for me," Tom sighed.

"Just for lunch, or for life?"

"For life," Tom said. He drank some tea. "I work some crazy hours, and I don't know when I'll get a vacation."

"You're a bad prospect as a husband," I said. "Unless you get a wife who doesn't care."

"Cops' wives don't seem to mind."

"They mind, all right. The sad part is police have a high divorce rate. Their marriages become occupational casualties."

"Didn't you ever want to get married?"

"I was married once. My wife died of leukemia a few years ago."

"Sorry, I didn't know that."

We were walking along 42nd Street toward the office when someone walking towards us gasped. He was looking beyond us. I turned and saw a car coming fast with a barrel sticking out of the front window. I tackled Tom, and we went down, sprawling on the sidewalk. The bullets flew over our heads. The man who had gasped, screamed and clutched his side. He went down. The car's tires screeched as it turned the next corner and raced away. Tom and I were on our feet. People had scrambled out of the way. I bent over the fallen man. There was a lot of blood. His face was pasty. He didn't even look 30.

A woman ran over. "What happened?" She was middle-aged and wore an orange colored waitress uniform.

"Call for an ambulance," I told her.

Tom grabbed my arm. "Let's get out of here."

We hurried away. "Did you see who it was?" Tom asked.

"I don't know who fired at us, but it was helpful Henry driving the car."

"Dutch's thug," Tom blistered.

"Let's pay Dutch a visit," I said, waving down a cab. We got into the cab and Tom gave the driver the address.

"Do you have a gun?"

"No," I said.

"Well, I've got one."

The Levantine was closed. We stood in front of the main entrance thinking for a minute, where to go from here. "Wait, somebody should be inside," I said. "Cleaning or counting bottles."

We found an unlocked side door. A man was behind the bar, putting ice in a compartment. He was a stocky man with brown hair. "Not open yet," he said.

"Is Dutch around?" I asked.

The man looked at us and decided he didn't like our looks. He put a scowl on his beefy face. "Who wants to know?"

"We do," Tom said, and produced his gun. "Come on out from behind the bar," Tom said. "And keep your hands where I can see them."

He did as he was told, but he wasn't scared. "Look I just work here, buddy," he said. "You got business with Dutch, you come back later."

"Is anybody here?" I asked.

"No. Nobody's here but me."

A car pulled up in front. There were footsteps. Somebody stuck a key in the lock.

"In the back," I said.

"No way," the stocky man said.

Tom pushed him, and the man went down hitting his head on the bar. We took him by the arm pits and dragged him to the back. It was some kind of storeroom. I let the man slump to the floor, then I heard their voices. Two men. One was Henry. "I can't believe you missed him," Henry repeated. He sounded bitter.

"We'll get him ..."

Tom and I walked out and Henry stiffened. He saw the gun in Tom's hand and slowly lifted his hands. The other man was tall and thin, and he stared sullenly at us. I extracted a pistol from each man and put them in my jacket pockets.

"Where's Dutch?" I said to Henry.

"You kiddin'?"

"Take this character into the back." I jerked a thumb at Henry's partner. I took out one of the guns, a .45, pointed it at Henry as Tom marched our would-be assailant into the back. I heard a crack, groan, a slumping thud, and Tom came back.

"You tried to kill us," I softly said to Henry.

"Naw. It was two other guys."

"Dutch sent you?" I said.

"What kind a game are you playin'? You know Dutch is dead. You blew him away."

I shot a quick glance at Tom, and peered back at Henry. "Say that again."

"You heard me."

"I didn't kill Dutch," I said.

Henry was unconvinced. "Yeah, right."

"When did Dutch get it?" Tom asked.

Henry did some sneering, and Tom shoved the gun hard under his chin. "When?" Tom demanded like an explosive drill sergeant.

"Sometime last night," Henry sputtered, "I found him at his place. All shot up."

"So you put two and two together and decided I killed him," I said. "So you and your friend came gunning for me."

"I ain't afraid of you wimps," Henry said. "If you're gonna shoot me, do it."

"Were you in Long Beach yesterday?"

Henry looked at me stonily.

"Where's the painting?" I insisted.

"If this guy wants to die," Tom said with feeling, "I'm about ready to accommodate him." An empty threat, but an effective one.

"You're gonna kill me anyway," Henry sniffed.

"Just tell us where the painting is," I said. "And nobody will hurt you."

"Dutch *had* it," Henry said.

"You know what it's worth?"

"I ain't stupid," Henry retorted. "I looked for it. Couldn't find it."

"Who do you think took it?" I said.

"How should I know? Maybe you did."

"I told you I didn't kill him. Was it Josephine—the lady with the black wig?" I pressed with increasing impatience.

Tom looked at me.

"I don't know." Henry squirmed.

"Who gave the orders? Dutch or the woman in the black wig?"

"Both. I think they wuz partners."

"Were you supposed to go yesterday?" I said. "Was yesterday the day for the break-in?"

"No. A week from today. I guess something came up and they changed the plans. All of a sudden we got orders to hit the place. That was yesterday. I asked Dutch how come, and he told me to shut up."

"Go, get in the men's room." I ordered.

Henry practically fled.

"What now?" Tom said.

"Let's get out of here."

A few blocks away I slipped into a phone booth and called Henderson's palace on Long Island. I asked for Sandra and was told she wasn't there. She was probably in the city. I then asked for Cora. Cora came to the phone.

"This is Lenny Cramer. I'd like to talk with you."

"Not now. My father is leaving his office early, and it's going to be bad. He's still fuming about yesterday. If you want to make a trip out here, I can give you a few minutes. But there isn't much I can add to what you already know."

"Uh huh. Do you know Dutch Selgado was killed last night?"

"I don't know the gentleman."

"He wasn't exactly a gentleman. I may turn up later in the day, Cora." I stepped out of the phone booth and Tom was waiting, looking nervous.

"The lady in the wig bit," Tom said. "You were talking about Sandra Henderson. Where does she fit into this?"

"Some day, when you come home with a good report card, I'll tell you all about it."

"Playing it close, huh? By the way, I found several more paintings that were sold to unoccupied storefronts. At least a dozen were sold to the same three or four addresses. Sandra the inside lady?"

"Figured it out, huh?" We started walking.

"Sandra stole Paul Manfred's gun; then lifts the key to the room where the paintings are, has a duplicate made and gives it to Dutch. It was Sandra all along. Did she knock-off Dutch?" Tom reasoned.

"You know some of it," I said. "Not all."

"Go ahead and be secretive. See what I care."

"The bad guys are falling out. I wonder who's going to end up with the jackpot?"

We took a cab to Marilyn's place in Soho and found Marilyn and Myra both there. Myra greeted me warmly, and Tom gazed with mock appreciation. I took Myra aside, and Tom began talking with Marilyn.

"Who do you think has the Turner?" I asked Myra.

Myra made her eyes round. "I don't know."

"I'm going to Long Beach," I said. "Why don't we all go?"

Myra frowned. "You know I can't go there."

"I don't think your father will make a scene when he hears what we have to say." I pronounced confidently. "There's been a lot of upheaval in his life. His prized possession is gone. He may never see it again. Come on, Myra, this may be a chance ... if nothing else you can do a little gloating."

Marilyn was furious. "That's a horrible thing to say."

"Yeah," Tom said. "That's a horrible thing to say." He patted Marilyn on the back of the shoulder. He was paying her quite a bit of attention.

Was it the first of May? I think it was. One day seemed to blur into another. I figured it was the last day of April or the first day of May. What did it matter? There was a time during my Ph.D. education program when I really wasn't sure which year it was.

"We're going to Long Beach." I was adamant. "Now come on. Everybody. Let's go."

Downstairs, we waited for a cab.

The second taxi to come down the street looked empty, and we stopped it. We piled in. I told the driver where we wanted to go. He balked. In fact, he was just heading for his garage. I stuffed a 10 dollar bill into his hand. "That's on top of what ever the meter says." He conceded, and we headed for Long Beach.

When we arrived Lloyd Henderson was upstairs in his sitting room and wasn't likely to come down till dinnertime. So Cora told me. She looked coldly at Myra and Marilyn.

"It's old home week," I told Cora. "I insisted they come along. I hate traveling alone."

Cora looked at me as if I was an insect. "What are you meddling with now, Dr. Cramer?"

"I just wanted to see the three sisters together," I said. The others weren't paying attention to us. Sandra had entered the room. Eyes made of dry ice. Silent. I took Sandra's arm, and we strolled through the formal garden by the side of the house. "Who has the painting, Sandra?"

"How should I know, Dr. Cramer." she said, venomously amused, in her precarious superiority.

"Dutch Selgado had it last. Somebody killed him for it. Who could get close to him without his getting suspicious? Some woman in a black wig?"

"Those are your questions, Dr. Cramer, so why don't you answer them yourself?"

"It was more than just stealing a painting, Sandra," I said. We stopped walking and we stood facing each other, under a maple tree, and behind her was a row of spring plants, bedded in black rich soil. "You and your sisters hate your father. You wanted out. So you came up with the perfect plan. Why not strike at the heart of the pain and steal what he treasures most? The Turner. It was all planned out perfectly, even to the date of the robbery. But I put a minor crimp in your plans. I found out what the target was. What you wanted to steal. It was the Turner. So you couldn't wait that extra week. The robbery took place the same day I discovered what the real painting was. And nobody knew that I knew, except Myra."

"And Myra informed us, so we went ahead with it the very same day." Sandra laughed haughtily. "You have it all figured out, don't you. How clever. I won't add or subtract anything Lenny. It's your story. Now all you have to do is prove it."

The haughty bitterness seethed like an adder's poison. Cold, calculating, cunning. The sins of the fathers? "There are three murders involved, Sandra. Somebody's going to pay."

"Sometimes you ring up the cash register and it says, No Sale."

Her smug arrogance gave me a sick feeling down to the pit of my stomach. "Where's Paul Manfred?"

"Paul who?"

"Your game is over, Sandra."

"Is it? We'll see." She leaned towards me. "You will stay for dinner, won't you? You and your charming friend? I'll arrange it with father."

"He's liable to throw you out."

Sandra patted my cheek over-confidently. "How can that bother me if I have $4 million in my hands? Or will have?"

We went back to the porch, and Tom took me inside the house. "I have it in my pocket, all wrapped up in a handkerchief. Spotted it at Marilyn's while you were busy talking. But what if it isn't the gun that killed Dutch? Myra will know I took it. You'll have some explaining to do."

"Don't worry about it."

Lloyd Henderson declined to come down for dinner, so one of the servants took him a tray. Before we left I went up to his sitting room. It was an enormous room, and he looked lost in it. He scowled at me. "Why did you bring Myra and Marilyn here? You know my wishes about Myra, and I can barely tolerate that Marilyn."

"I thought you had a soft spot for Marilyn?" I stood by the side of his posh, leather recliner. His eyes seemed sunken but alive, animated. He was a hardened old bird.

"Just a spark," he murmured. "Just a spark." He twisted his head, looked up at me. "What about my painting?"

"Dutch Selgado had it last. He's dead and someone else now has it. One double-cross after another."

"You'll get it back for me, won't you?"

Somehow I almost felt sorry for him. Then again, I wasn't his kid. I told him I was a forensic accountant. He hired me to investigate Marilyn's alleged financial chicanery at her mother's art gallery. I told him how fake paintings were being sold to non-existent customers.

About my suspicions of drug money being transferred to Selgado in the form of fictitious loan repayments. He shook his head angrily and muttered something that sounded like a combination of vicious frustration and abject contempt. I left him.

Sandra drove Marilyn, Myra, Tom and me to the station and didn't wait for the train to arrive. She waved her hand and drove back to the house, back to her father.

When we got off at Grand Central, I got another cab for mother and daughter, told Myra I might call her later, and then Tom and I went back to the office. Only the night man was there, reading a magazine, the ***Journal of Accountancy***. Said his daughter was studying accounting. A good profession. I agreed.

We went into my office.

Tom unwrapped the gun on my desk. It was a .38 caliber Smith & Wesson revolver. He put a pencil through the barrel and lifted the gun, looked at the spent powder on the edge of the chamber and sniffed. "Yeah," he said. Which meant it had been fired recently.

I wrapped the gun up and put it in a drawer of my desk. "You owe me a handkerchief," Tom said.

"Where did you find it?"

"In a drawer under some sweaters," Tom said matter-of-factly.

"Let's talk."

"Sure." Tom settled in the client's chair in front of my desk.

"You found the gun in Marilyn's flat. So Marilyn gets the brass ring ... unless her mother planted the gun there. But I doubt it. Daughters will throw their own mothers to the wolves, but mothers are a certain kind of breed. It's not likely a mother would sell her own kid down the river."

"Where does this put Sandra? Or Josephine?"

"Sandra is right there, up to her neck in murder, up to her neck in grand larceny. I don't know if she did the actual killings, but she was behind it, all right."

"And Cora?"

"Cora, too."

Tom shook his head. "You're guessing."

"If the gun you found today is the murder weapon, the one that killed Dutch, then Marilyn will talk. Even part of a print should do the trick."

"Who killed the two artists, Noren and Walker?"

"I think it was Marilyn."

"She killed her lover?" Tom was skeptical.

"There were millions involved," I told Tom. "Marilyn's share would come to a million or more. When people are into crack, they get irrational." I massaged the back of my aching neck. "The artists knew what they were doing with the fake paintings and they knew about the upcoming theft," I said. "Either Marilyn told them about the theft in an unguarded moment, or she wanted to recruit them as fall guys in the robbery. On the other hand, maybe they were taking revenge against all of the men they used and abused, and had used and abused them over the years."

"You're still guessing."

"It all fits. You checked it out yourself. You told me there was no stealing from the gallery, only signs of using it to launder the drug money."

Tom grimaced. "Some Columbo—raincoat and all. It fits nicely so it must be true."

"You go and talk to Shirley. I want to talk to Myra, without Marilyn around."

After Tom left I dialed Myra's number. She answered on the fourth ring. "You're alone?"

"Yes, Of course. I gave Marilyn a couple of Advil and went home."

"What's with Marilyn?"

"She—uh—doesn't feel too good."

"Something she ate ... or drank?"

"Your friend, Tom—did he search Marilyn's apartment?" she asked.

"Yes."

"I see." There was a tense pause. "What are you going to do?"

"I thought I'd come over and talk to you."

"All right, Lenny."

I slowly hung up the receiver, thought for a moment, switched the light off and left my office.

161

Fifteen

Performance standards are essential to a management principle known as management by exception, *which states that management should devote its scarce time only to operations in which results depart significantly from the performance standards.*

—Gordon Shillinglaw

Myra tried to look calm, but her hands were trembling. She poured coffee into mugs from a porcelain and chrome pot. We sat in the living room, and her eyes studied me. "Marilyn didn't kill Dutch or anyone," she said. "I did it all. All myself."

"Sure."

"I was with you when you found out that the Turner painting was what we were after. I warned Sandra and Cora, and so they did the robbery that same day."

"You were the one who *told* me about the Turner," I reminded her. "You didn't really want the robbery to take place, did you. You thought if the others knew I had found out they would call it off. But they didn't."

I sipped some coffee. "How could they? They were in too deep already with two murders on their hands. And it was more than greed that was driving them. It was hatred. Hatred, and 30 years of seething resentment for a father that treated all of you like disrespected trash under his feet. A father that gave the love and acceptance you deserved to useless, deteriorating relics, and to his own vein, material idols. I thought you were in it too, Myra. But no. Your father gave you a raw deal, but you couldn't hate him. In spite of how deeply he had hurt you, he was still your father. The others did though. Cora and Sandra. And they had a willing ally in Marilyn."

"You don't know what you're saying," she protested.

"I'm sorry, Myra. I'm no shrink. I'm just calling it like I see it. You didn't want Marilyn to get involved. So you asked your father for help, hoping some private eye or lawyer would stop them. Instead he called me. I'm sorry I didn't get to the real issues sooner, but I was thrown off by the ruse about Marilyn defalcating assets from your art gallery. It's not easy to fight family hatred and greed. Cora and Sandra wanted revenge. They were sick of looking after your father—giving, giving, giving, and being stepped on like insignificant fools in return—day after day, year after year, for 30 years. You were stronger. You got out years ago. They didn't. They must hate him, and hate themselves now beyond what you and I can possibly comprehend."

She lifted the mug of coffee and then put it down. Her eyes were wet. "I can't believe it all got so out of hand. Teddy and Bram were never even a part of it, and now they're dead. I'm not going to worry about that Dutch Selgado. Sooner or later he'd have been caught in his own dirty meat grinder. Marilyn got involved with the wrong crowd and it's all my fault."

"You think it's that simple? Come on, Myra. Your sisters and your daughter made their own choices. They took their chances, and they lost. Where is the painting now?"

"I don't know."

"It has to be hidden somewhere."

"You want to search the apartment? Go ahead," she said curtly.

"It wouldn't be here," I said. "They don't trust you anymore, do they."

"They knew how I felt. But what was I supposed to do?" Her face was distraught, intense strain around her eyes. "Report my sisters and my own daughter to the police?" She was just almost screaming at me. She was beginning to lose it—practically on the verge of hysteria. "There was nothing I could do." She spit back at me.

I didn't argue with her. Three murders. Up to their necks in crime. And there was nothing she could do. I drank some coffee, but it had the taste of something bitter, corrupt. I put the mug down. "Will they brazen it out?"

"I don't know," she shook her head, looking down. Her whole body was trembling.

"Have you got any more aspirin? Why don't you take some and go to bed."

Her eyes were glistening with tears. Her mascara was black streaks running down her cheeks.

"It was Cora and Sandra. They pressured Marilyn to go along."

"Did Marilyn let it slip to the artists," I said. "Is that what happened? Or did she hate Teddy as well—was he exploiting her—abusing her—or was she jerking him around? I don't imagine he was a very strong personality."

"Yes. One night after an unusually wild party Marilyn was high—almost out of her mind. Bram was there. She spilled the story to Teddy in front of him. The next morning she knew she had made a blunder and went running to Sandra. It was Sandra who decided Teddy and Bram had to be silenced."

"And Marilyn obliged," I finished sardonically. "Easy enough for her to kill her love-hate crack-head boy friend. And then Bram Walker had to go. Why did she stop there? Why didn't she kill Masters too?" Myra was sobbing heavily.

"Frank wasn't there the night when Marilyn blurted out about the robbery. But Teddy or Bram could have told him. So Sandra had Dutch scare Masters out of the country." She dropped her face into her slender, sweating hands.

"Then Marilyn killed Dutch," I pressed relentlessly. "She took the painting. What did she do with it?"

"I don't know. I don't know," she insisted in a panic, crying now uncontrollably. "I asked her. She wouldn't tell me. She probably handed it over to Sandra or Cora."

"They wouldn't keep it in the house on Long Beach. They're not that stupid."

"I don't know where it is Lenny. I swear I don't." She struggled to regain some element of composure.

"All right, Myra." I put my arm firmly around her. "It won't help if you get hysterical. Marilyn's a big girl." I held her by the shoulders and looked directly at her face. "She went into this with her eyes open. She was looking for big bucks, and it didn't work out." I stood up slowly. "There's no winners in this dirty game, Myra. Only losers."

She didn't see me to the door.

The next morning, in my apartment I started on the phone. I finally located Detective Richard Steele. I asked him to meet me in my office in an hour. He agreed. There was something about him I respected. Something you can't really explain.

I shaved and showered and was in my office in 40 minutes. When he arrived I gave him the gun. "I think it killed Dutch Selgado. That'll be up to your folks in ballistics. There may be prints on it. Marilyn Riley is the one you'll want. She also killed the two artists."

"You'd better give it to me straight."

And I did. I laid out the whole sordid mess to him. It had finally come to a head. And the stuff was pouring out in torrents. Cora, Sandra and Marilyn—I talked about the hatred, the greed, the murder. Steele took the gun away after talking about concrete evidence. It was now up to ballistics and the fingerprint experts.

I sunk into an emotional depression. It scared me to think I had actually started getting sucked into the whole web of lies and manipulation myself. Tom had been right—I was being played like a violin, suckered into withholding evidence, misleading everyone, including myself, thinking I was helping my client. The claws are subtle, and I realized I was no more immune than the next well-meaning sap.

Hildy dropped a fax on my desk, but stayed away. She saw my mood.

Tom came in later and talked about Shirley. He had talked with Shirley late last night.

"The poor kid's out of a job now," he informed me. "The Levantine is closed down. I told her she'd make a great administrative secretary."

"It would be an experience, wouldn't it?" I said flatly.

"What are you moping around for?"

I told him what I had dumped on Richard Steele.

"And you're convinced Myra wasn't part of the whole plot?" He sounded skeptical.

"Yeah. Very convinced."

"You sure you haven't been taken in by her? You'd feel like a sucker if you found out she was just trying to save her own hide, still playing you for a jerk."

I said nothing.

Tom sat down and stretched out his long legs. "You're a smart auditor in a lot of ways, Lenny. Real smart. Even for a Ph.D. But you have a sentimental streak that'll get you into trouble in this tough racket."

I looked up at the corner of the ceiling and saw that the spider's web was gone. Someone must have noticed it, and had used a broom.

I hoped the spider hadn't been damaged. If it was the stubborn kind, and might still be alive and kicking, it would rebuild its web—somewhere.

Could Lloyd Henderson rebuild his web without his daughters? He was no dummy; he had to know they hated him. Did he even suspect they were behind the robbery of his painting?

❋❋❋

There was a memo from Hildy on my desk after Tom and I came back from lunch the next day. I returned the call and soon was talking to Richard Steele.

"The homicide boys called me. They can work fast when they feel like it. Ballistics checked that gun. You can pick one up on the street for 50 bucks. The bullet that killed Dutch came from that gun, and the prints on it belong to Marilyn Riley. An assistant D.A. is getting out a warrant. Can't do anything about Cora and Sandra Henderson unless Marilyn sings. Are you sure Myra Riley is out of the picture?"

"Confident."

"And the painting?"

"Maybe Marilyn will confess. Who knows? I don't know. Can't even guess. We got a fax from Sotheby's—confirms one of the paintings sold through Myra's gallery couldn't possible have been genuine. Different owners, different buyers, different prices. All within the time frame Sotheby's had the original in their possession."

"Well, my boys gave Dutch's place, the Levantine, a complete shake. From top to bottom. No paintings. No forgeries. But some interesting stuff. Five kilos of crack, some boxes of paraffin, and expensive laboratory scales. In the basement. Dutch's murder has nothing to do with me. I'm only assigned to recovering that painting. I have two or three good informants. So far, nothing. That Turner is being kept under wraps."

"It'll show up."

"They don't always show up," Steele said. "There are millionaire collectors in Europe and South America. They thrive on owning rare art—the kind no one else can have."

"Will you let me know if Marilyn gives a full confession?"

"As soon as I get the word, I'll call you."

"If I'm not here, I'll be home." I hung up and took two aspirin.

It was so neatly tied up. All I had to do was pick up my marbles and go home. Some forensic accounting case. That is, if Marilyn talked.

And if she did talk, then what? Cora and Sandra rounded up. A trial by jury. Pretty strong case, they'd be convicted.

My part was over.

Or was it?

The painting. The Turner. My client's stolen asset.

Where was it?

I picked up the phone and called Myra. "You'd better go over to Marilyn's. She's going to need you for moral support."

"I'll always hate you for this, Lenny Cramer."

She said it in a steady voice. No hysterics. She meant it. Why?

"Talk to her, Myra. Find out what she did with that painting."

"That's all you care about."

"It could help her with the judge." Who was I kidding? Three cold-blooded murders.

"You're just looking out for your client," she reasoned, sounding betrayed. "You don't care about Marilyn ... and you don't even care about me."

"Okay. So stay away from her then."

She slammed the phone down.

I was feeling some of the ache. It stung, and I felt abjectly alone in that office, not even the spider for company. An hour later I said good-bye to Hildy and went home.

I took a cordless phone into the bathroom and got into the Jacuzzi. Hot water jets cascaded the back of my neck in the tub, and I tried to just put it all out of my weary mind. When the phone rang it was Myra, not Steele.

"I saw Marilyn." Her breathing was heavy. "There was no painting in Dutch's apartment. There was a fight, a shouting match—and she shot him. She admitted it to me."

"Did the cops get there yet?"

"I—I don't know. Marilyn just ran out and took off. I went after her, but I lost her."

"Where are you now?"

"In a booth on the street. Uh, ... Prince Street."

"You'd better get home. If the police talk to you, please don't mention that we talked."

"Why should I do you any favors?"

I could lose my tenured job at the university. "You can't hate me that much Myra. You did go to see Marilyn like I asked you."

"Yes. I—I don't know what to do."

"Go home Myra. Stay out of it if you can. You've got to pull your own life back together. You can't help Marilyn now."

She hung up and I got out of the tub, dried off, put on my blue pajamas and gave up any idea of eating dinner. I was hungry, but I didn't feel like eating anything. I got a

Pepsi and sat in front of the TV set. I didn't turn it on; I just sat there and drank the Pepsi from a coffee mug.

I shouldn't have called Myra. If she talked, the police might think I had used her to warn Marilyn. I was in trouble if they thought that. We all make stupid mistakes. The road to hell is paved with good intentions. The better idea is not to make the mistake in the first place. That's not always so easy.

It was late when someone rang my door bell. I put on my bathrobe, and opened the door. Richard Steele walked into my foyer. We sat down, and he didn't look too friendly.

"Two detectives went to get Marilyn Riley," he told me laconically. "Guess what? She had flown the coop. One overnight bag gone. They caught up with her at the Port Authority. They hauled her to the D.A.'s office. In half an hour she told them everything. Her aunts will be picked up tonight. Some judge is being chased down to issue the warrants."

"All's well that ends well," I said with a feeble grin, feeling like my face was made out of scrambled eggs.

"How did she know we were after her?" he wanted to know.

"That's easy," I said. "She knew Tom Reardon found her gun, and she knew we would turn it into the police. So she took off. What else would she do?"

Steele seemed to relax after that. But one can't be sure with police. Especially one as sharp as Steele. He went on, "I talked to her myself about the Turner painting. She said it wasn't in Selgado's apartment. Maybe. My boys went over it, up and down. No painting. Could be she got the painting and stashed it with someone else."

"Know what I think?"

"What?"

"I think Dutch was double-crossing the sisters and their niece. Why should he do the dirty work, then split three or four million bucks with them?"

Steele shook his head. "What have we got? Three dead men and a missing painting. When are you going to spill everything?" he said.

"Look, I'm not holding out. Why should I?"

"I won't push it—for now." We walked to the door and we shook hands and he went away. I finished my, now flat, Pepsi and went to bed. My head felt like I had crashed into a brick wall.

❂❂❂

"The last roundup," Hildy said when I walked in the next morning. "It was in the morning papers. Cora and Sandra Henderson and Marilyn Riley. The police have them in custody. And that's not all. Mr. Henderson called up early this morning to talk to Johnny. Our firm has been fired."

"I hope Grant's not too broken up about it." I said and went into my office.

"There's a memo on your desk," she called after me. "Phone message."

I picked up the slip of paper. All it said was Washington Square Park—12:00.

I sat down and leaned back and closed my eyes. I felt I had done a lousy job. It had been a merry race, all right, but it was coming to closure and I had left behind a very dissatisfied client. I had done my best. If his daughters are a bunch of murdering thieves, he can't blame that on me. The acorn doesn't fall far from the tree. At least, he still has one honest daughter—the one who got out from under him first.

Hildy stuck her head in the doorway. "Tom wants to know if you need him for anything this morning."

"No. Not right now, thanks."

I got up and felt sluggish. Downstairs, I had a cup of black coffee. It helped some, not much. Tasted more like gasoline.

I walked quite a way before I stopped by a bus stop, and climbed on board one vehicle that took me to the Village. There was plenty of time but it was a warm day, and I needed some sun. You can't beat a park bench for that, in the city anyway.

I don't know how long I sat before Paul Manfred appeared. He was wearing a sleeveless denim jacket over a bare chest and looked like one of the Village locals. He grinned at me and sat down beside me.

He told me he didn't owe me anything, and I agreed to that. His grin went away and he looked solemn. "Henderson is getting what he deserves. He stepped on all of us. It was Cora who put the idea together. Get him back where it'll hurt the worst. The dough and the possession he cherished most."

"Why did you bother with the 50 grand?"

"That was all I wanted. It was enough for me. It was Sandra that brought in Dutch. She needed him. Dutch collected the 50 grand, and when he handed it over to me he said I was a sap, and that I would owe him big time. I'm not greedy, understand, but when I was on the loose with the cops looking for me, I went to Dutch for help. I should have known you couldn't trust him for anything. Instead of handing the painting over to Marilyn, he wanted me to hold it—in the dump apartment where I was staying on the Lower East Side. When things cooled down and the painting was sold, Dutch would split with me. But when Marilyn didn't get the painting, she blew Dutch away in a rage. I guess by that time she was thirsty for killing—no one was going to stop her from getting what she was after."

"You have the Turner?"

"Just told you."

"Maybe you already sold it."

"The collector they set up to buy it doesn't live in the good old U.S.A. He's somewhere in Europe. Don't ask me exactly where. I'll get there. I'll find him. That's why I'm talking to you—help me get out of the country, and I'll cut you in for half."

"Not me, Jack. You have 50 grand. You'll manage. Only I don't believe you're going to Europe. My guess is South America."

"When I sell the painting, I'll send you a postcard."

"Forget it. I'd rather not hear from you."

"Look, I didn't steal the painting. Dutch gave it to me."

"Give me a break. You're in possession of stolen property. Maybe Henderson got what he deserved, I'm not his judge. But there's blood on that painting—three men. You think you can live with that? You'll never get away with it, Paul. Look, isn't there enough greed in this world without you adding more to it?"

"Why don't you call the cops then?"

"I just might. I don't feel like playing the hero today. This is my day off. I'm tired, Manfred. I'm tired of this case. I'm tired of you. You do whatever you want to do. And don't send me any postcards."

"I just thought you'd be wondering what happened to the painting. So, now you know."

"Not my concern. Henderson fired our firm."

Paul Manfred stood up and stretched. "I'm not a mug anymore. I know that much."

That's what he thinks. I watched him walk off. Under the arch and down Fifth Avenue. I watched until he was nowhere in sight. The sun was warm on my face. One more call to Steele, and Manfred was done for. Did he really think I would help him? My back ached. I was getting hungry.

I found a phone booth and called Myra. Yes, she would have lunch with me. Why not?

We met in Bryant Park and walked till we found a cute little French crepe shop. We ordered, and she ate some of her blueberry and cheese crepe. It had white powdered sugar on it. I ate everything in sight. I was more famished than I had thought.

"My father lost two of his daughters, and I've lost my daughter. It's so unfair."

I was out of talk, so I didn't say anything.

"It was all a nightmare," she said.

I sipped chocolate-almond flavored cappuccino.

She looked at me. "My father called me. He wants me to come and live with him."

"What are you going to do?"

She looked faded. Her eyes weren't bright at all. Her grin was a terrible, pasty thing to see. At least, I thought so.

"I'm going to live there with him," she said. "I have no place else to go."

I cringed, and sipped the last of my cappuccino.

❂❂❂

Too often senior managers assume that by mechanically eliminating chunks of business or consolidating operations, they will improve the Company's position. In fact, only by designing controllable and highly integrated manufacturing processes—something we call robust—can companies lower overhead permanently and, at the same time, remain viable broadline manufacturers.
—Mark F. Blaxill and Thomas M. Hout